WOMAN WITH DARK HORSES

stories

by

AIMEE PARKISON

WOMAN WITH
DARK HORSES

AIMEE PARKISON

2004

Starcherone Books
P.O. Box 303
Buffalo, NY 14201
www.starcherone.com

Grateful acknowledgment is made to the following publications in which some of these stories were first published:

Other Voices: "Baroness with Strange Eyes,,; Crab Orchard Review: "The Upstairs Album,,; American Literary Review: "Corolla,, and "The Last Secret Tour,,; Fiction International: "Smile, That's Why He Loves Her,,; Harpur Palate: "Collecting,,; River City: "Blue Train Summer,, and "Textures,,; Quarterly West: "Van Windows.,,

Cover Art: George Oswalt. Cover Design: Betsy Frazer. Layout: Geoffrey Gatza. Editor: Ted Pelton.

Library of Congress Cataloging-in-Publication Data

Parkison, Aimee, 1976-
  Woman with dark horses : stories / by Aimee Parkison.
    p. cm.
  ISBN 0-9703165-5-0 (alk. paper)
  1. West (U.S.)--Social life and customs--Fiction. I. Title.
PS3616.A7545W66 2004
813'.6--dc22

                              2004002980

TABLE OF CONTENTS

I

BLUE TRAIN SUMMER

When I first saw the dead girl from far away, she looked like a
blue sheet strung out beside the tracks. I came closer to see what
the men were running from and discovered the sheet was a dress
covering her face and hands. She was like a gift to me, my first
real dead girl, someone to remind me of what it was to be alive
and make me feel fortunate for breathing. Even though I was in a
melancholy mood and fighting a hangover, I knew there was a
slim chance that I wasn't the one who killed her.

Certain moments were somehow lost. Just before
sundown, the evening sky had been full of light. Pink-hued
clouds shadowed the white moon. I was drinking apple wine
when I drove my old Cadillac into the field, then fell out the open
door and decided to sleep in the wheat.

At first I couldn't remember why I woke on the ground
beside my car. My face was pressed against the grains by the time
I decided to get up. It took me a while to locate myself, crawling
along the ground to the edge of the crop line to find my car and
remember where I was.

After the men ran away, I was left alone with her. This
was southern Oklahoma in the seventies. She was wearing a
robin's-egg blue dress with pale yellow, lazy-daisy embroidered

socks, no panties. One of her bright black-heeled shoes was missing. Her lips were dry like wood, and dirt was scattered through her long brown hair. When I pulled the tangled strands away from her face, I saw her eyelids shimmered with silvery green powder. Where her dress was torn off her shoulders, a necklace glistened. It was made of fake gold beads like the necklace my sister Karen once owned. I knew if I started to scratch at the beads some of the thin golden paper would fleck away, revealing the white plastic core.

Her blood looked like old paint, a dark rust color that matched my car. It seemed as if she had been splashed in that odd color, so natural against the red dirt showing through the tire tracks beside her. The dirt and the blood mingled together in places near her breasts and legs. Some of the dried blood was built up in layers and textures like a painter's canvas showing the difference in depth between nearer and farther forms. It was as if some sort of abstract painting had been begun on her dress and body. Her face and hands were the only large patches of canvas that had been left untouched to let the brightness show through.

In the wheat where I found her, the Cadillac's doors were wide open, the seats covered with locust wings and papers, the radio blaring static broken by stray music. Somehow my car wasn't ever far away from me. All those nights of highways, I had bathed in gas-station bathrooms after eating fast food behind the wheel.

But in the field, I wasn't in any hurry to drive off, even though I knew better. A long train was coming. Before I saw the first cattle car glistening in the sun, I heard the whistle blow.

Crescent Street met Thomas Street nearby. A red pickup stopped in front of the tracks as the wooden gates crashed down.

The high school was on the other side of the tracks. The parking lot behind the blond-brick auditorium was empty. School was closed for summer break, but in the football field behind the parking lot, the team practiced their plays, lining up in tight formation near the goal posts. I could hear the coach yelling, but I couldn't make out what he was saying. His voice was drowned out by the train whistle.

The train looked blue in the distance. It was a beauty, sleek and bright, going faster than it had seemed when it was far away. I stepped past the girl and thought about jumping one of the cars, but I changed my mind at the last minute. I didn't want to travel with a bunch of dazed cows, and I was afraid of leaving the girl behind.

Looking back, I think I was a fool then, and I'm embarrassed to say what I thought about the girl. She was mine, but not like a baby or a sister or even a lover would be. In the whippoorwill's call, I thought I heard a woman's voice and knew this dead one was her own and yet also mine. In the gray-blue eyes that were drying on the wind, half-closed, I could see that she was with me but also far away. She saw me, and yet she didn't see me. Maybe she was like most women that way. On the streets, I could walk among them and not be noticed. As I touched her hand, she could not feel my touch. We could have been just two bodies, except that I was more than my body. So was she, at one time. That is why she was not entirely there. In the broken wheat where we lay, she had a name that did not follow her into that field.

Now, thirty years later, I'm ashamed. I pretend I came from another town, drove a different car, went by another name, attended a different high school, and was never in the field with that girl.

After flinging oils onto my palette, I paint in a closed room in complete darkness, no lamps or candles, no windows to let in streetlight. Working with a palette of rust, slate, earth, umber, burgundy, dust, red dirt, and yellow wine, all on a background so blue it could be mistaken for sky, I don't even know what I'm doing.

I will not know what I have painted until I open the door, removing crumpled rags from slight cracks in the doorframe, letting in the dawn.

In the dark, everything I render is so abstract no one could know she is a girl. She takes on no definite form but is released into colors of her hair, her skin, the wheat, her blood, her cheap necklace, and silvery makeup mixing, blurring, and bleeding into hues of her dress, the sky's tone threaded into the gray of the passing train.

Sometimes while painting, I convince myself Karen was not my sister, just a girl in my dreams, wandering through the darkness at the edge of the field to race trains in the night, then hiding in the bedroom closet near her old dresses, her legs covered in sweat that would not wash away, leaving no visible wound beside the trail of bruises marking her thighs.

That purplish trail led to a place I would never know. The next morning, we acted like nothing had happened, even though the bruises still remained.

I was always good at pretending. Maybe I should have been an actor or even a lawyer. I might have done something outside of dark bars along country highways. Perhaps I could have preached to runaways and drunken men, offering salvation in exchange for words. People I barely knew might have treated me with respect, and strangers might have thought I was someone worth talking to.

On the road, anywhere I drove, every stranger was a friend. Even though I could talk for hours to people I didn't know, I never had much to say to the people I used to know.

At dawn, opening the door, I discover all the colors of the girl have blended into a violet gray wrapped in warped ovals of charcoal, rose, and pine, shaped like the age rings inside of a cross-section of a fallen tree. In the first light, I know all I've been doing is painting her bruises, fading.

For years, I spent my evenings committing various small crimes across the county. So much of what happened was just on a lark, games I played instead of spending money.

Was arson a symptom of disillusion, trespass of loneliness? I don't know. My vandalism might have been linked to guilt or boredom. If I was brave enough to sign my name on someone else's building or a bridge that belonged to all who crossed it, I could not be the coward I feared I was. And if I was not a coward, how could I feel guilty and ashamed?

Maybe voyeurism was a sort of painkiller and aphrodisiac rolled into one long glance though a lit window, narrow in the night. Shadows obscured my face, and in darkness I found such sweet disguises.

Regardless of what I had done, I had been waiting to find a body, but I thought it would belong to a live woman, someone who could separate herself from her physical being – a stripper, or a woman of the night – she who could talk without speaking, she who could say more with a flick of her wrist or a flutter of an eyelash than words could ever mean to a man like me.

Sometimes when drinking, I blacked out and couldn't remember what I had done. Most of the time, I was sure I hadn't done anything but wandered through alleys and slept under bridges. The real question was what people had done to me while I was in that lost state.

Once, when I came out of it, I was under an overpass, lying down next to the cars swerving to miss my head. My wallet was gone. People were yelling at me, and I couldn't figure out where I was or how I had gotten there. A lot of signatures were scrawled across my arms in indelible ink.

Another time, I suddenly found myself in a Baptist church in the middle of a Sunday service. In a glass case full of blue water, in front of the entire congregation, a preacher I had never seen before baptized me. He put one hand over my nose and another hand behind my back, then dipped me into the water. Before I knew what was happening, I was choking, but not for air. The man was not afraid to touch me. He was smiling as the congregation cheered, and I was sobbing, clean for the first time in a long time. And Karen came back to me in my dreams, her face and hair glistening in the murky water.

Something about being so close to the train made me recall the way that water trembled as Karen pulled me up to the pond's surface so that her face was gleaming above mine.

In the field, the ground shook as I knelt near the girl, letting the train pass us by. The wheat trembled with the force of it. Because the train was so long, its vibration lasted enough time for me to think it was coming from her.

We were too close. I knew the danger of being seen by the engineer. While I held her, I was trying both to comfort and conceal her. I thought she was moving beneath me. I kissed her ear.

She was gone and had been gone for hours. Her body was growing stiff despite the sun's heat that warmed us. I knew that I would eventually have to let go.

After the train moved on, I still listened for the sad sound of its passing. I rolled off her. Then I looked to the football field.

I could see the players and was worried that they could see me. I couldn't recognize their faces, only their blue jerseys and their blocky forms. Still, I worried they might think it odd to see a man watching them from the wheat. To conceal myself, I stayed crouched beside the girl. Since I was somewhat hidden, I decided it was a good time to continue my examination.

The girl's lips were hard, but the inside of her mouth was still moist. I pressed her mouth open to examine her braces. Then I closed her mouth and started to shiver. But her mouth wouldn't close all the way, and her braces were as cold as her teeth.

One of her arms rested neatly over her chest. The other arm was twisted behind her back. At first, I figured there was something strange about her hands, the way the right hand was holding the left hand so tight as if she had been afraid to let go of her own fingers. Maybe she was extremely double jointed, I ventured, attempting to bend her arm at the elbow. That's when I realized she was in an impossible position. Because of the way her arms were placed, there was no way humanly possible for her hands to be holding each other.

Her right hand was attached to her arm that was resting over her chest, but the left hand was not connected to her body. It must have been severed at the wrist, I reasoned. After gently elevating her by lifting her shoulder, I reached behind her back to feel her left arm. That's when I pulled back the rest of her dress and discovered her left hand was still there, attached to her wrist.

The hand she held could not have been her own. I don't know why I couldn't have seen it before, this obvious detail escaping me simply because of the way the wrist was draped in a delicate fold of blue material.

I saw it, but I didn't want to see it.

When I unlaced her fingers from the hand, I noticed she wore a ring that was missing a stone. Letting my eyes roam the farther ground behind me, my gaze weaving through the stalks, I saw a speck of violet glass glinting in the sun and crawled along on my hands and knees to fetch the stone back to her, just to see if it would fit in her ring. That's when I saw the other girl, the one without a hand. On her stomach, she lay face down in a puddle of mud and leaves, a dark trail marking the footpath as if she had been dragged through the grasses. I knew there was a possibility that she, too, was Karen, but that was a possibility I couldn't bear to consider.

When I was seventeen, I thought I would get a day job that would allow me to pose as a newspaper reporter while all along writing about the crimes I committed under another name. That was the "big plan."

Mostly, in the early days before the "big plan" fell through and I moved on to the "little plan," which was no plan at all, I stole – a car from a rich man, a huge plastic blue hippo from a tire store, and a glider from a traveling theme park.

I had decided that I wouldn't return to my family until some newspaper hired me as a reporter, but no newspaper ever hired me. The editors said my descriptions were too florid, not professional enough, and full of glaringly inaccurate details, which in reality were more accurate than they could have ever known or imagined. So I lied to my mother on the phone and started working at a grocery store thirty miles away from my hometown. Karen wouldn't talk to me then, even on the phone. Just as I stopped returning my family's calls, I moved farther away and got an unlisted number so my father couldn't track me down. Even if he wanted to, I assume he never did. We rarely spoke to each other, even when we were living in the same house.

I got promoted from sacker to cashier, but I was too involved with my night crimes to let my day job get me down. I broke into strangers' houses and rearranged the furniture. I painted a white room green and a blue door red. Romance lingered on beery air, shadows of oak leaves in streetlight. Women never even knew I was there, crawling beneath their windows, trying to avoid shifting my weight from one boot to the other. The crunch of fallen leaves could give me away.

Then, for no reason I could figure, I started to think about Karen and couldn't sleep at night. Her face was in every portrait I painted on the grocery store's blank back walls. Her voice was in the wind. She was just eleven years old when I left home and would turn seventeen that summer I came back to town. I knew I had to see her again when I started drinking the apple wine.

Maybe that was why I ended up so close to the high school, which had been a meeting place at night when I was younger.

I was never invited to meet anyone, and I didn't know anyone to invite, so I crouched in the dark and spied on the others. I saw couples coming together in the fields – boys and girls, students and teachers, cousins. Mostly, I watched their hands, how they held each other.

Lonely for years, I kept telling myself there were too many people in that school. The district lines had been moved three times in four years, changing and dividing the town into strange shapes that meandered crazily on local maps like the ants that were walking over her face.

Keeping the flies off her mouth, eyes, and hands, I thought of all the crippled animals I had tried to save and how I couldn't also be with the other girl, the one who would have to be forgotten – a goat with bent legs, a duck with one wing, a three-legged cow, and an unfortunate swan whose long, knotted neck was twisted dangerously, so close to the Texas border.

Although I never told Karen what happened to me while we were kids, somehow she knew. I had a hard time imagining her as a student, the same age as I was then, walking the high school halls.

I guess I never knew much about her, but she knew a lot about me. She was just a little girl who was too smart for her own good, and I was just her older brother – a messed-up kid with too much going on to notice she had secrets of her own.

One evening, I almost said to her, "Hey, I'm one of the ugliest kids at school because of my face!"

It was true. Some kids barked like a dog whenever I passed them by. So what if I wasn't exactly living in the jungle? I knew my place just the same: I was like that weak animal the lions picked off from the herd to make the herd stronger.

Some kid I never even knew punched me in the nose and broke it in three places so that even when it healed it never looked the same. Karen used to watch me at night when I changed the bandages, in case I needed help.

Later, I asked the kid, "Hey, what did I ever do to you?"

For a second, he looked confused. Then he just glared at me and said, "I don't know, but you probably did something."

As he turned to walk away, I started to take the bandages off my nose to show him what he had done because he was a liar and I still wanted him to be my friend. Every time I saw him after that day, he made a fist like he was going to punch me if I came too close.

Karen was waiting for me in the parking lot the day he decided to have another go at me.

"Please," she said, stepping right up to him, in front of me. "Don't hurt my brother."

And, for some reason, he didn't. He just looked at her and walked away.

People were always hitting me for what I didn't do while ignoring what I had done. At night, I thought if I murdered someone, I could probably get away with it, no big deal. But if I tried to love someone, people would think I had done something wrong.

When I heard the rumbling sound coming from the dead girl's belly, I tried to ignore it, realizing it was beyond her control and nothing to remember her by. She could belch without moving, but there was something moving inside her. So I held on.

Karen could stay oddly still. She could look into my face without blinking and hold her fingers over a candle flame without flinching from the heat. Taking a straight pin or a little knife, she could cut herself without hesitating, wiping away her own blood as if it were water. No one could stop her, not even me.

Perhaps I wouldn't recognize Karen if I saw her, or maybe she wouldn't recognize me. We would be two strangers coming together in the wheat, a young girl stumbling upon a drunken man in the field at night, looking through the windshield of his empty car, wondering why it was abandoned there, waking the man, not noticing him until she was within his grasp.

The girl might have been waiting for someone in the parking lot the night she died. She might have been chased into the field. She might have been hiding in the wheat all along, playing a game with the other kids or waiting for a lover. She might have been running from someone she knew, a friend or a father. She might have been lost while trying to escape him.

And finally, when there was no one left to escape but me, what could I do to harm her except for look and just keep looking, as if even after she had died, there would always be something about her worth seeing, something I could not pull my gaze away from. Long after I let go, I held her with just my eyes and I would have gone on holding her, if I had been brave enough and knew of a way.

When I examined the dead girl's arms, I found a small red heart tattooed on her left shoulder. A thin arrow was drawn through that heart. Underneath the tattoo, the scrawled letters carved into her skin read NOBODY'S GIRL.

My eyes started to water when I lay on the ground beside her. I wanted to give her another name. For a moment, I thought I was going to cry, but I stopped somehow. Even if she was my sister, I knew no matter how long I sat beside her, I could never figure out who she was.

THE UPSTAIRS ALBUM

Frances awakened in the upstairs, her room smelling of fried chicken. She had grown accustomed to the ease of her fingers slipping through the raw meat and the soft assurance that as long as she stayed in her room there would always be plenty of feathers in her pillows.

She was the first one. She was skinny and she was hungry and her body was covered in fine, black hairs. She was sixteen, and so were the twins, her cousins, Sheri and Brandi.

Frances wanted to escape the house in Alabama. She had lived with her grandmother for two years, helping with the household chores ever since her parents' divorce.

The twins had arrived only a week ago. They had ridden in the back of their father's blue pickup. Everything they owned fit in four cardboard boxes. Frances had watched from her bedroom window as the twins' father quickly unloaded the boxes, waved to the twins, and drove away. She wanted to go with him, but it was too late.

At first, the twins ignored Frances. They arranged the upstairs furniture so the beds faced different walls. Linen sheets and tattered blankets were strung from the ceiling to form three small rooms and a center where a large, gray dog stretched out on a tiny, yellow sofa.

Sheri covered her wall with photos of Brandi placing lighted candles inside of a carved pumpkin, pretending to pray in front of a famous cathedral, leaning over a fountain, and twirling in a white dress. Brandi hung her collection of antique mirrors framed in shapes of leaves.

Around the window, Frances had pasted a collage of magazine photos of the ocean with houses on the shore, couples running on the beaches, and stretches of pink, teal, and gray water touching sky. Tonight she studied one portrait of a woman digging into the sand with her toenails while her hands held a white starfish up to a crescent moon. Her bathing suit was made of three perfectly formed sand dollars tied together with leather cords. Her eyes looked up to the starfish in her hands so that Frances could see only the blank balls of her eyes with the irises hidden under the lids. On her skin and in her hair, pale sand shimmered like rain.

By nightfall, beyond her window, Frances heard dry grasses tangling on the wind and the hush of hens roosting on the low roofs. She imagined men laughing in the rooms beneath hers and her grandmother turning in her small cot, her bones popping in their sockets like wood on fire.

Frances closed her eyes and then opened them to look at the photo of the pale woman in the darkness, her skin dazzling the light on the ocean. With her fingers, Frances plucked and twirled the curly hairs on her arms. She listened to the hairs turning until she heard other sounds.

The mirrors had been darkened for hours when Sheri began to cry out, as if from a dream. Frances rose to discover what had happened. She brushed past the blankets hanging from the ceiling, entering Brandi's room in silence. She found the twins in Brandi's bed, asleep in each other's arms.

In the morning, Frances saw the twins standing together outside Brandi's room. Brandi smiled and waved gently with her fingertips. The blankets hanging from the ceiling were pulled apart like curtains opening onto a mirrored stage where Sheri stood still, moving only her head first to look at her sister and then to look up at the pink globe on the ceiling.

Because the twins were blondes, Frances, with her black hair, automatically became the dark one when she found herself near them. On the bed behind them was a black album Frances took for a secret journal. She was still getting used to living in the midst of the twins, their perfumed hair falling around their heads like the soft metal wound around their wrists and ankles. She hesitated to disturb their privacy. But the twins' voices clanged together like the bracelets sliding over their arms. The scream in the night stayed with Frances, as prominent as the black album on the pale linen of Brandi's unmade bed. The sheets were tangled and molded by the shock of two bodies sliding apart.

From the sofa, the dog Charleston, part Great Dane and part Doberman, looked Frances straight in the eye as the twins slipped past him. Frances looked away from her dog and suddenly felt the shame of her long body towering over the twins.

"Did you hear something last night?" Frances asked. She reached out to touch Sheri's elbow. Frances felt the three-pronged bone jutting out of Sheri's skin. Sheri looked at Frances strangely, and Frances realized that perhaps no one besides Brandi had ever reached out to touch Sheri's arms before.

"Did you?" Sheri asked. She began to pull away, but Frances held on tighter to her arm.

"Nothing," Brandi said.

"She's just skin and bones," Frances said, finally letting go of Sheri.

Brandi reached out and grabbed Sheri's wrist. "Sweet Jesus," she said before releasing her.

The twins ran down the narrow staircase, laughing. Brandi moved as easily as bubbles blown out of the hole at the end of a plastic wand. Frances heard their small feet tapping softer and softer as she ran her fingernails over her arms.

Charleston yawned, a rumbling that could have come from the pit of Frances's own stomach. When she turned around, his head was bowed down to her legs and in his teeth was the black album.

When she opened the album, she expected to find a secret account of what the twins thought of her and her dog, but it held only photographs of the twins from a long time ago. She turned over the faint impressions of two identical faces and of two girls wearing the same polka-dotted dresses. All the photos of the twins before they could walk showed that the sisters once looked exactly alike. For a moment, Frances rested her face in her hands. She knew that now no one outside of the family would believe Sheri and Brandi were sisters or even the same age. Ever since they moved into the house, Sheri had begun to say, "We were once twins." Frances thought Sheri wasn't trying to distort the truth but was only trying to explain what had at last become of her and her sister.

The twins no longer wore the same clothes, nor did they have identical faces unless they were walking under different light. Sheri's features had become cynical, so hollow and severe that many times Frances thought her eyes were set more in a skull than in a face. The starved look and the black shawls Sheri wore made her appear much older than she was, while Brandi twirled around the house like a young girl in white and yellow dresses.

On the last photograph in the album, Frances saw a woman's finger looming large in the frame, as if the twins' mother had accidentally touched the lens just before she snapped the shot. Frances put her own finger over the one in the photo. The two fingers were exactly the same size.

Aside from the black album, Frances had seen Sheri resemble her sister only once. Just before entering the house, Brandi had knelt over a patch of green berries in a shaded wood as Sheri stepped out of the trees into the light. In that moment, Frances couldn't tell Sheri and Brandi apart. But that was the last time she could have mistaken one twin for the other.

Frances closed the album on the two sisters with the same face, wondering if the album could reveal why time had worked so quickly on one sister while leaving the other unscathed.

In the kitchen, Brandi said, "Hey, Frances, would you get that jar off the high shelf? Thanks."

Frances handed her the jar of pickled okra.

"Now," Brandi asked, "would you open it?"

As Frances turned the lid, she glanced at the corner where Sheri was sorting silverware in a tray. Over the sink, Frances's grandmother was deboning a chicken.

Frances handed the open jar back to Brandi.

"Hey, Sheri," Brandi said, "isn't it nice to have Frances in the kitchen? With her around, we don't even need a man to do the strong stuff."

"Thanks, Frances," Sheri said without looking at either of them. She was getting careless with the silverware, slinging it into the tray. Frances knew that the clink of the knives made her grandmother nervous. Frances's grandmother began dropping wooden spoons and whole pieces of raw chicken onto the kitchen floor.

"Trust me never to eat again," Sheri said, her eyes moving from the floor to the grill.

"You want to exorcise the living ghost of Jesus from this ragged body?" Frances's grandmother asked Sheri as she reached for a floppy piece of chicken, as loose as the skin on her arms. She ran it under the faucet and flung it onto the hissing grill.

"I won't have one of my girls starving in my kitchen," the old woman often said, as if she suspected Sheri's gaunt figure would reflect badly on her cooking. "What will people say when they see the bones on that girl popping out? I won't have Sheri tainting the food. Over my dead body, I won't have her mixing death with everything I do to keep you girls alive."

Sheri suddenly emptied the silverware onto the floor. "I

won't eat any of this," she shouted. "You can't make me. I know things about your precious granddaughter and her creepy dog that would make *you* want to die."

Frances was afraid of what Sheri might say.

"Honey," Frances's grandmother said more gently, "what can I do to convince you?"

"Leave me the hell alone," Sheri said.

"Do something," Frances said to her grandmother.

"There's nothing to do," the old woman whispered, looking out the window where the hens scratched through dirt in the backyard.

"I want out of this damn kitchen," Sheri said. She picked up the vat of hot grease. Then she smiled at Frances's grandmother and hurled the grease into the air. It sizzled and smoked as it splattered the floor and the wall behind the long table where the girls usually had their dinner.

Frances's grandmother looked at Sheri in disbelief.

Frances reached out to touch Sheri's face. She put her hands in Sheri's hair to steady Sheri from her grandmother's wrath. A gob of Sheri's brittle hair broke away on Frances's fingers. The grease was burning whole sections of the blue wall away, leaving a bed of naked hollows that seemed as random as a sore.

"Get your paws off my sister," Brandi said.

Frances saw her own hands as large and steady as those of a man who worked out in the fields. She had always seen her hands as masculine. She had even been proud of their strength. But until that time, she had known nothing wrong with that type of hands, even when they finished off a woman's arms.

In August, when Frances's grandmother converted the house into a bed-and-breakfast, she had it painted a pale, liquid green Frances associated with the ocean before a storm. Even though it had only four rooms for guests, the bed-and-breakfast became famous throughout the town for the quality of its dining. Frances was often hungry because the more the customers ordered, the less her grandmother fed her and the twins.

Country-fried chicken was the only dish ever served. Every noon the house held men's laughing voices echoing off every wall. Because of the way the chicken was prepared, grease coated the walls with a clear film that would not wash away. Frances blamed the grease for the glasses of ice water that slipped through the customers' hands. She spent her afternoons on the floor, mopping up shards of ice and glass.

In the dining room, sunlight reflected off chandelier glass, then glanced off Brandi's painted fingernails while she placed two baskets of biscuits onto a table where four men were seated. She poured ice and water out of a carafe and into tall glasses.

Leaning against a greasy wall, Frances drank a glass of water. Her body and her clothes were always greasy, drenched in sweat. She drank the water down and poured herself another glass while Brandi waited on the tables.

Frances was able to slack off in the dining room because she was officially the one who slaughtered the chickens. Sheri was the one who cleaned the bodies, and Brandi was the one who placed the baskets of fried legs, thighs, and breasts in front of customers at the tables draped in red cloth.

Once when the men were busy eating, holding chicken and biscuits and glasses, they complained of having no free hands. Brandi unfolded the cloth napkins away from the silverware that would not be used and placed the napkins around the men's necks as they looked up at her appreciatively and scooted away from the table.

Many times before, Brandi had been warned by Frances's grandmother not to cause confusion among the customers by mentioning that Sheri was her identical twin. But Brandi couldn't resist telling stories about herself and her sister. She was a sixteen-year-old girl who waited on ravenous men. She innocently brushed crumbs off strangers' shoulders, looked at the men with clear, steady eyes of no particular color, and seemed to take for granted the extraordinary sleekness and pale color of her long hair as she talked about Sheri.

Frances always dreaded the moment when the men asked to see Sheri, perhaps expecting Sheri to be as beautiful as her sister. Sheri was terrifying to strangers, so she kept herself hidden in the kitchen unless someone called for her by name. Once when a man asked Brandi to introduce her twin, Brandi carelessly touched his hand as she reached for his empty glass. Before the two hands had separated, Sheri stepped out of the kitchen doors with her lusterless hair pulled back into a bun twisting the skin on her forehead away from her skull.

When the customers first saw Sheri, they dropped the chicken back onto their plates. One man even spilled his glass of water. Sheri was soaking wet, and loose feathers clung to her arms. Frances could make out every bone and thought what a perfect model Sheri would make for an anatomy class to study the human skeleton as it surfaced on a living body.

Sheri ground her teeth at the men, and her displeasure was so undisguised that a man broke the silence by saying, "Excuse me for living and for trying to eat my lunch in peace."

Brandi motioned for the men to go on eating, but they wouldn't. Sheri did not move nor did she look away. A fat man put a finger into his mouth, slowly pulled out a long, thin bone, and waved it at her with a smile. "Waitress," he said, "check." He and the rest of the men rose from their tables.

Frances followed Sheri to the backyard. Sheri chased the hens, but she could not catch them. When Frances saw what Sheri was doing, she wanted to help. Once Frances caught the birds by their necks and legs, they did not fight or even move. One by one, she captured them and handed them to Sheri, who tossed them high into the air. Frances looked on in amazement, thinking what strength Sheri still had left to be able to throw living birds so far. They landed on the low tree limbs. They did not fly away or attempt to come down. Instead, they clung to the branches and stared below them.

"Why does it take them forever to come down?" Sheri asked as she looked up at the trees.

"Got me," Frances said, her arms feeling tired, muscled, sore.

"Everything takes so long."

"I know."

"She touched his hand forever."

"I know."

"What's going to happen to us?" Sheri asked. The birds moved their heads from side to side.

Frances thought there was something strange about time and hunger – that the hungrier people became, the faster they aged, but the slower time went by.

These were the exact words she wanted to say to Sheri. Instead, she said, "Whatever."

At eight o'clock in the evening, the girls arranged themselves around the long, wooden table in the kitchen. Brandi and Sheri sat on either end so they could watch each other eating. Frances sat on the long side, studying the grease-scarred wall.

In front of Frances, in red baskets and white paper, the food the customers had not eaten was splayed out in narrow rows. She was starving, but she sat patiently with only her eyes shifting from the food to the twins. Brandi reached for the basket of chicken, and Frances remained calm, thinking that no matter what had happened, in the past, there had always been some chicken left for her. She closed her eyes, knowing that Brandi would take the best portion for herself and leave the rest for her sister. Brandi chose the breast, then slowly passed the basket to Frances, who hastily grabbed the legs and left Sheri with the wings.

Sheri began to eat slowly, stripping the wings clean by

sucking on the bones. Frances tried not to stare at Sheri as she ate. To divert her attention from the twins, Frances searched the blue wall marred by grease for patterns the way other people searched clouds. She saw hands reaching for hands, women's heads with their long hair in disarray, and hands reaching through the hair. The moment she found a panther leaping, she looked down and realized there was no more food on her plate.

"You can have mine," Sheri said, holding her plate out to Frances.

"Sure you don't want it?" Frances asked.

"No, you take it," Sheri said, looking at Frances's outstretched arms. "I'm not hungry."

"You never are, are you, Sheri?" Frances asked, while gnawing on a wing.

"For God's sakes, Frances," Brandi said. She rolled her eyes at her sister.

Frances knew when to be quiet. She let her eyes wander over the stains on the wall. The panther was in the left upper corner. Below the panther were a tall bird with its neck bent as if drinking, three moons, a witch's skull, a bridge over water, and a black bird landing on a child's hand.

The window behind Sheri was open, and through the screen Frances heard the dark sound of the hens roosting in the backyard, the muffled disturbance she often mistook for the hush of falling leaves, wind through the grasses, or a tug on a long skirt. Just when the light had no color, the birds lined themselves up in neat rows along the fence tops and the low roofs, but in the morning they would scramble for the last pieces of filthy corn and then peck at one another's eyes.

"What are you looking at, miss?" Brandi asked, running a paper napkin from one corner of her mouth to the other.

"For a minute," Frances said, quickly making up a lie, "I thought there was someone out there. That's all."

"That's all," Sheri said.

A pile of bones, gray and jagged, lingered on the plate before Frances. Her eyes searched the wall. A tall man's dancing shadow . . . Jezebel; waves on the ocean and fingers caught in a woman's hair . . . Jack-o'-lantern, the face of a child in prayer . . . Another cigarette thrown down; a leaf on the wind . . . Two sisters and a panther leaping.

Balls of Sheri's hair rolled along the floor like tumbleweeds barreling down Baker's Road. Brandi kicked her sister's hair away from her toes.

Living with the twins, Frances had learned to hate the thick, coiled strands of her own hair. She took the loss of Sheri's light hair particularly hard. What a shame, she thought, that she could not pick Sheri's hair up off the floor and sew it back onto Sheri's head, or maybe even onto her own.

Trying to disguise the bald spots on her head, Sheri wove the bottom layer of her hair onto the top of her scalp.

Brandi sighed as she ran her fingers through her own hair, which was so light and so fine that it separated into translucent strands glistening like mayfly wings beating in the moonlight.

When Brandi turned off the lights, Frances sat on her own

bed beside the wall covered with pictures of the ocean and the open window taking in country breezes. She took off the screen, and Charleston leaped from the fence to the chicken coop to the low roof and from the high roof into Frances's room. He settled into her bed as if it were a place he belonged. When she held him under the covers and whispered secrets into his ears, he lay beside her like a young man who could close his eyes and not be afraid of her leaving.

Touching her fingers to his mouth, Frances told him about houses on the ocean shore where shark teeth would be strung together and hung above doors for wind chimes. "You and I will wade out into the water, and there will be beaches where there once were only fields. I'll catch more fish than you and I both can eat, so we'll never be hungry."

Frances put her lips to his ears while she studied the portrait of the woman holding a starfish in the moonlight. Then she turned away from Charleston and reached for a package of matches on the windowsill. She struck the first match, and the warm light picked up the blue in Charleston's eyes. With the second match, she began to singe the hairs off her arms.

She heard Sheri call out, "Fire! That's brilliant, Frances. Burn it all down."

Then the night was quiet again, except for a soft murmuring from Brandi's room. Frances wondered what the twins said to each other when the mirrors went dark. She walked into Brandi's room and found Sheri in the shadows of her sister's arms. Frances heard the muffled sounds of Sheri screaming into a pillow as she ran her hands up Brandi's shoulders to the face that used to resemble her own.

"Go back to bed, Frances," Brandi said. She had her hand on Sheri's head.

Frances left Brandi's room and went back to Charleston. He lay very still as she whispered, more still than any human would ever lie next to her, almost as if he were afraid to breathe and the biggest secret was just the sound of her voice as she asked him, "Charleston, what are we going to do now?"

Frances's grandmother had a face a young girl could get lost in. Her wrinkles were etched so deeply that Frances wanted to run a finger through the lines to see where they would take her. Without risking a finger, she guessed all creases led to the mouth.

"I'm not blind, even if you think I'm an old woman," Frances's grandmother said, pounding the ruined kitchen wall with her fist.

"I don't," Frances said as she sat down at the table and put her face into her hands.

"I see how things are going with you three."

"What do you mean?"

"Honey, I'm trying to save you. Stop following those girls around, even if it's just with your eyes."

"I don't know what you mean."

"They come from evil, and now they're getting nervous."

"I don't know anything about them."

"I didn't want to tell you, but now I don't have a choice, do I?"

"I'm listening."

"Now that they look nothing alike, their parents can't stand them, what with Brandi more perfect than they ever hoped a child could be and Sheri worse than they ever imagined."

"She just needs to eat. She'll be all right."

"She has been beyond that for ages. A long time ago their mother walked into a room with a ribbon for Brandi's hair. But Sheri was the one standing at the window. Was it my place to tell her? How could I know what would happen? When Sheri turned around, their mother screamed, '*Brandi, what have you done to yourself!*'"

"I don't want to hear anymore."

"Then she put her fingers into her mouth and bawled out loud. Ten years ago, the first time she realized she would have to give up both daughters to pay for what she had done."

"Who put that idea into her head?" Frances asked. She had no idea what her grandmother was trying to tell her. She only knew that something terrible had happened to the twins a long time ago, and she suspected that her grandmother had played a part in it.

"She couldn't afford to feed and clothe two girls, so she almost let Sheri drown once." Her grandmother swallowed hard.

"Where did you hear that?" Frances was alarmed by the serious expression on her grandmother's face.

"This was when the twins were still little things, both still perfect. Early autumn. She was alone at her husband's farm."

"What was their mother's name?"

"It doesn't matter. But she filled a tub on the porch with

water, poured in a sack of apples, and plucked her girls down inside."

"You mean they were bobbing for apples?" Frances began to suspect that her grandmother was making up the twins' story as she went along. She smiled at the old woman, no longer frightened by her words.

Her grandmother nodded her head, as if acknowledging the smile. "A heavy one sank to the bottom of the tub, and Sheri put her head down under the water to retrieve it. After she had been under for a long time, Brandi began to whimper, and their mother went inside to pour herself another coffee."

"Stop it." Frances slapped her hand on the table, tired of what she assumed were ugly lies. But her grandmother kept talking.

"I was there the whole time, hiding, ready to save Sheri if it came to that."

"Did it?"

"Hush, why don't you? No more questions." Her grandmother reached out and smacked her on the arm.

"Okay." Frances touched the red outline her grandmother's palm had left behind.

"Halfway out the door, the twins' mother was ready to pull one lifeless child out of the water and to hush the other's screams. But things didn't turn out the way she thought."

"It could have been an accident," Frances whispered, realizing that every time her grandmother had told her an awful story there had always been some small truth in her grandmother's words.

"Halfway out the door, she dropped her coffee onto the cement steps. Brandi was pulling her sister's head out of the water with her teeth. . . . And you don't believe a word I've said."

"How could I?" Frances laughed under her breath.

"Well, I'll prove it. Look for a half-circle scar on Sheri's forehead. You have to get close now that Brandi's teeth marks are faded white."

"I'll never get that close."

"Don't be so sure about anything. You just keep looking, and maybe you'll see what I've seen."

By the end of summer, Sheri had become nothing more than a vision hinting of Brandi's eventual demise. When the two walked with their groceries along Baker's Road, they moved more like mother and daughter than sister and sister. Frances saw them moving beyond her. She thought Sheri appeared to be the much older woman, hunched over, but refusing to let the younger carry the groceries along the way.

Frances and Charleston caught up with the twins easily because Sheri had to stop on the roadside to rest, her breath coming fast and shallow. Brandi put her arms around her sister. But by then, Sheri was just a frail thing, bones with the hair that was still attached as colorless and brittle as the autumn grasses breaking off in the wind. Sheri stood still, leaning against Brandi.

Nervous that the twins were falling too far behind, Frances walked back to them. Sheri smiled pleasantly as one grateful to be momentarily held by her sister. Both of them clung to each other, their arms laced together.

"Come on," Brandi said, "we're too young to be this tired."

Frances put her arm around Sheri's shoulders. The three walked back to the house, where in the kitchen chicken sputtered on the grill, sounding like rain.

Sheri did not set a place for herself at the table, and Brandi seemed not to notice. Brandi took her normal portion, then left the rest for Frances, who dumped the entire basket of chicken onto her plate and let her eyes scale the wall as her teeth picked the bones clean. Trees. A tall man's dancing shadow. Fingers caught in a woman's hair. A naked girl rising out of the water.

Sheri fell asleep at the table. Brandi reached out as if to shake her sister awake but picked up a tiny folded napkin instead. She ran the napkin over the corners of her mouth, rose from the table, then left the kitchen and some food on her plate.

When Frances reached out for Brandi's plate, Sheri did not stir. Frances touched her shoulder, and she did not open her eyes.

Sheri was still asleep when Frances picked her up and held her in her arms, carrying her up the narrow staircase, imagining Sheri looked like a fragile bride dressed in black.

Frances put Sheri down on the bed carefully so as not to jar her bones. Then Frances looked at her own arms and the hairs, which had grown back longer and just as curly but now darker and coarse.

She began talking about the ocean but suddenly felt that once she got there, she would not be a girl much longer, nor would she ever become a woman.

"Charleston and I will take you with us," she said as she smoothed Sheri's hair, which came off in her hands. "You won't have to do anything but just lie back on the tip of our sailboat."

To awaken Sheri, Frances opened the window, and the wind that blew through the grasses came inside to lift Sheri's hair away from her skull. Her clothes were so loose that they began to fall off her body. Frances looked away from her, and out the window she saw the shadows of hens roosting on the low roofs. She thought how the inside of a woman looked the same as a dead bird that had been bled, plucked, and carved into long pieces.

Brandi walked into the room and found Sheri still sleeping.

"Now look what you've done," Brandi said, taking Sheri away from Frances by awkwardly lifting Sheri in her arms.

Brandi began to lose her grip. Sheri's head fell back hard, and Frances noticed a light scar, the white arch of a crescent moon, on top of Sheri's forehead.

"Now you've got her confused," Brandi said, looking out the window. "Now she probably thinks the winds tearing through the grasses are waves on the ocean. For God's sakes, Frances."

Sheri's eyes began to open, but by then her irises had already rolled back into her skull until where her eyes used to be were only vacant spaces picking up flecks of moonlight.

Brandi whispered over the moonlight in her sister's open eyes, "Don't believe a word she says. We're nowhere near the water."

TEXTURES

With a flashlight in hand, I climbed the attic ladder behind my father and heard the clatter of my daughters running through the halls below us. The dolls' suitcases of gowns were small, easily lost under the rest of what we had decided to store out of sight. They were somewhere buried under ruined blankets, my mother's wigs on their blank Styrofoam heads, and the handlebars of a bicycle. My father had to make his way through my mother's faded wedding dress crumpled on the rafters, her huge hair dryer, her rusted sewing kit, and a seat torn out of the back of an old car. He kept kicking doorknobs that rolled around loose on the floor until they collided with lampposts or the dismantled grandfather clock strung out beside a cracked mirror. There was a space in a corner where a tiny rocking chair lay on its side. The dolls were stacked behind it.

My daughters loved those dolls after I washed and ironed the doll clothes my mother had designed and sewn. I had to throw away the ballerina's mink shawl, practically devoured by beetles.

When the girls held the dolls, they didn't know any better, but I knew there was something wrong. The difference was in the repulsive texture of the hair. The dolls' hair didn't look like hair anymore. There was no sheen to it, like an old woman's hair dyed rigid auburn. Twenty years ago, the last time I had brushed that hair, it felt like a baby's fine curls.

Each doll had a name, and my daughters kept the names I'd given them: Chatty Cathy, Katrina, Julie, Mitsy, and Bobby.

Cathy had a string in the center of her back with a ring on the end to slip your finger through. Pull the ring, and she told you her name or asked for yours. She could only say so much.

Katrina was the ballerina. Mother had sewn her sophisticated clothes – mink shawls, velvet shawls. She had no tutu or ballet slippers. You could see specks of glitter through the clear plastic of her miniature high heels. She was always dressed for the opera, never the dance recital.

Then there was Julie, the baby doll, larger than the rest, but younger. Her hands were forever posed in that moment when an infant reaches out for its mother in the direction of her voice but grasps only air.

Mitsy was a Barbie Doll – a fake. You could tell the difference in her weight. She was too light. Her body was a thin, plastic shell filled with air. I had to be careful with her because I knew a careless hold could force the curve of her breasts back into her body or snap a leg off her tight hips.

Bobby was the soft doll – a body of white muslin, her clothes the replica of my pajamas when I was five – periwinkle polka-dot pattern on flannel. But that doesn't matter because Bobby was the one my father never found.

*　　　*　　　*

My daughters, Ashley, Launa, and Mady, combed water into the dolls' hair to soften it, but the hair felt dry even when all wet. The dolls fell apart in my daughters' hands. I know now it was only my gentle touch and afterward my neglect that had held them together all these years. First, Ashley came to me with the ring off Cathy's string. The string just kept going into the hole in Cathy's back until there was nothing to pull anymore. We lost it. There was no other way to make the doll talk. Then Mady bit Julie's pinkie off, and Ashley snapped Mitsy's right leg off. Really, I didn't mind. Launa liked the sound Katrina's ankles made when she moved them at the joint – telephone ringing under a pillow, taut strands of hair snagging on the brush.

When I was in the fourth grade, I stopped playing with my dolls. I remember dressing Chatty Cathy for the last time. I closed her suitcase, and that was that.

"You're sure about this?" my father asked when he finally put the dolls up in the attic. Of course I was sure. But if he had asked me why, I wouldn't have known why I quit the dolls. Now I know the reason. Even as a child, I felt too old to play house. I was a woman in a child's body. I didn't need plastic children.

I hated to see the dolls cracking, their eyelashes plucked away, their heads balding. I began to realize the dolls were older than my daughters were. The dolls were my age, and I couldn't stand the thought of them outliving me. I couldn't bear to think of the dolls being passed onto my daughters' daughters and to further generations after I was gone.

Maybe the girls' father, Donny Jacobs, never even knew the dolls existed. He lived and worked on construction sites. He helped pour the foundations of our church and house. In the evenings, he would come home in a daze, exhausted and slumping down in the couch. He was too tired to look at me or to speak to the girls. Then one evening he just didn't come home. I never saw him again, and I don't expect I ever will.

To pay the bills, I began working the night shift as a part-time nurse at the local hospital. I drifted in and out of my daughters' evenings and only saw them on the weekends. They stopped asking for their father and let me sleep during the days. They learned to take care of each other.

Once in the early morning, I found the three of them in a small circle braiding each other's long hair. They were so solemn they didn't know I was there. I went back to my room in silence. I wouldn't be surprised if they had gotten used to living without me the way they had gotten used to living without their father. We barely noticed each other.

If my mother had been around, that never would have happened. I never could have forgotten her so easily. Mother had spent her nights sewing lace onto miniature pantaloons, knitting doll socks, and embroidering symmetric designs onto the fronts of dresses. She had closets full of material dyed in pastels and various shades of beige. Because she made my clothes, material was the one thing my father would let her buy. He was tight with the money he gave her, and it was hard for her because she liked to keep herself looking as immaculate as the dolls she gave me.

She always had to have the latest fashions and shoes to match the exact shades of every dress and a purse to go with the leather of every pair of high heels. Once a month she frosted her naturally auburn hair to a silvery blond. Those were the worst days when the bleaching solution might sting her eyes. Mornings I watched her put on makeup. She reminded me of a woman in a porcelain mask – only her hair and her eyes showed through. She was meticulous with the tight rolls of her curlers. This was the transformation she had to go through before she walked out the door.

At the church luncheons or at the ladies' houses, she was a different person – charming, the type of woman who makes the other women feel gorgeous even while they appraise the cunning perfection of her lip liner.

She tried to teach me these things, how a man wants more than one woman. Because a wife has to know the art of transformation to keep her husband, my mother taught me that it wasn't enough to be one woman; she and I had to have the features of many. Like her, I had to know how to change the color of my hair and my eyes just like I changed my panties at night. I knew how to live in a silent house and be the talk of the town, how after thirty years of being a brunette I was smart to bleach my hair platinum blond. My wardrobe changed with the fashions, and the fashions obeyed the cycle of seasons.

Makeovers were my mother's religion. She taught me about masks of facial cream smeared on at night and washed off so I could put foundation on in the morning. I had to powder my neck until the puff met the collar of my blouse. I hid the skin I showed. Hose and gloves disguised my hands and legs. I grew up knowing ladies never wore white shoes after Labor Day. I was careful about the white shoes, but I never had a handkerchief when I needed one.

I didn't want my daughters to feel ashamed of their bodies and think that they had to hide themselves like I did. So I moved with them to a secluded house out in the lake country where I let them run around naked in the backyard. They liked to sunbathe on the patio and wash their hair with the garden hose. Mady, the youngest, was the first to regret this. The girls were in their swimsuits and running under a sprinkler in the front yard. The sun was out, so they lay on the end of the warm concrete driveway to dry off afterward. There were bits of dirt and grass and leaves tangled in Mady's hair and sticking to her legs. She skipped to the garden hose to wash, took off her swimsuit, and went to lie back down on the end of the driveway. She must have fallen asleep out there. Ashley and Launa were already in the house by then. We heard an engine rev, and Ashley, Launa, and I ran outside to find Mady crouched in the corner of the garage. We asked what was wrong. She wouldn't tell us at first. Then she said that two men had driven by on a motorcycle and seen her sunbathing in the nude. She was only five years old, and those men were laughing, not jeering, as they sped away.

*   *   *

Mady never lives anything down. But when I was five years old, I was different, practically invisible. I was a good girl, and nothing really terrible ever happened to me. I had only one phobia of my own, and that was toilets. I always hated to go to the bathroom, so I tried to hold it in as long as I could. My father used to count the squares of toilet paper on the rolls after I finished, and he scolded if he thought I used too many.

One day I flushed the toilet and the water in the stool just kept flowing. I waited for it to stop. Then I got scared and called my mother. When she saw the toilet, she started screaming for my father. He took off the lid on the back of the toilet and reached in to get this black rubber ball out of the water. I never knew it was back there, and I didn't want to know what he was going to have to do with it.

Later that night, I was calling for my mother again, and this time she wouldn't come to me.

She could ignore me like that. When I walked into a room, she decided whether or not she could see me standing there. There were days she wouldn't make dinner and days she wouldn't talk to my father. She locked herself in her bedroom and made doll clothes.

Once I stood outside the bedroom door and listened to my parents.

"Just tell me what I did wrong," my father would say to her. She was probably sewing the diamond snap on a tiny shawl.

"If you don't know, then I'm not going to tell you."

"You don't even know, do you? You don't fool me. You know it's not true."

"You think I imagined it, what you did to me?"

"Don't do this to me again."

"I can't believe you," she would say, probably before she put her face in the pillow.

They were arguing in the car one night, and I was in the backseat. The road was dark, and the next thing I knew my father stopped the car, got out, and started walking. Mother scooted over to the driver's seat, and the headlights were hitting on my father while she was driving. Of course, if he were really leaving her, he would have told her to get out of the car and left her on the dark road. It didn't happen that way, but I think she would have loved him more if it did. As it was, he heard my voice calling him back from the window. He turned around and walked to the car. My mother moved over so he could get back in the driver's seat, and he drove us home.

Sometimes I wish he had shoved her out of the car. The headlights hitting her legs and shoulders would have been a spotlight for her. She would have basked in that drama and adored her shadow lengthening before her on the pavement. If my father would have tried to run her over, she might have run back to him. She might have put the tip of her tongue on the edge of his chin just to taste the thrill of a man who thought she was important enough to be murdered like a woman in the movies.

How could he have known she was like that? To this day, he confesses he still thinks of her as not one woman but two – the one he thought she was and the one he married.

He told me he met her at a church picnic after he had just gotten out of the military. He came from a long line of preachers and felt fortunate to meet a church-going woman who looked the way she did. Years later, he would say he should have known better, that no woman could spend that much time on her hair before going out on Sundays and still expect the congregation to think about God while appraising her high curls. She used to play the organ while the choir sang, so she was right in front of the congregation during the service. Every Sunday before beginning his sermon, the preacher would compliment her on her playing. "My, Grace, that was lovely." One Sunday he forgot, and she never went back to church again.

But on that day of the picnic, when she had her white dress on and the tablecloth spread out underneath her and it started to rain, she just laughed and ran to my father's car. He noticed how the other women were screaming at their fiancés to hurry up and unlock their cars, cursing their husbands for not saving their white sandals by carrying them over the water, or arguing with their brothers over how close to hold the umbrellas over their heads.

"Why didn't you think to bring that umbrella?"

"Where's my rain bonnet? I know it's here somewhere. Look what this is doing to my hair!"

But not my mother. She was tranquil, and by that he knew she was the only one he wanted.

That's how she got out of the cigar factory where she worked before he met her. She was the secretary there and brought the men coffee and powdered-sugar donuts. Those men smelled of sweet smoke and would never have the money it took to marry a woman like her, so they just smacked her on the behind whenever she passed them by.

Well, as my mother used to tell me, at least they noticed her. But she didn't like to go home smelling of the wrong kind of cigars. It made her dizzy, and now that I'm a nurse I know what all those years of second-hand smoke might have done to her. If my father hadn't met her in time, she wouldn't have escaped lung cancer. She probably wouldn't even be breathing now if he hadn't come along.

I imagine her washing the smoke out of her hair at night when she was still young and beautiful. Maybe she regretted washing away the scent of those men like she regretted washing away her makeup. The water exposed her real face to the mirror and made her seem plain.

Maybe that was the problem she had with my father. Like the preacher's son he was, he disguised his desire. He didn't kiss her on crowded streets in the pouring rain. He didn't smack her on the behind whenever she bent over to pick up socks out of the hamper.

I think she sometimes realized what she was doing after their fights. She would come out of her room and say to him, "I don't know how you put up with me, Frank." Then she would walk back to her room and shut the door.

Sometimes my father made me go to her at night. I would be afraid of her anger, but I knew she wouldn't hurt me. Sometimes she'd flinch when my hair fell over her face before my lips touched her cheek. Sometimes she'd talk to me, but I wouldn't want to hear what she was saying.

"You're lucky. My own mother tried to kill me – jumped off a porch while she was still pregnant with me. Are you old enough to know what that means? I don't want to live in a world where I'm not wanted. . . . "

I was only a child when I realized I couldn't help her. So I decided to become a nurse, to comfort the sick, and to devote my life to helping others. I wanted to have daughters of my own just so I could tell them I dreamed of them before they were born.

My daughters have never seen my mother. I was nineteen and about to go off to college when she disappeared. Things had been normal at home. She didn't spend as much time in her room then. But without telling me or my father, she hired an attorney. The next Monday the deputy sheriff served divorce papers to my father at his office. The sheriff told him he couldn't go back home, and that night my father climbed through a window to get some important papers and the vacuum cleaner. A month later, my mother had her divorce and her settlement, fifty thousand dollars.

I imagined what that money was to her then – earrings, snag-resistant pantyhose, wigs made from the hair of college girls who needed cash, tailored dresses, new coats any time she wanted.

She just took off with all that money and moved to the far side of the city.

Seven years later, I saw her phone number was back in the local directory. I thought I would just call her to tell her I had another daughter. She never answered the letters I had sent her, and I wanted to know if she was getting them.

"Well," she said, "that's just great, Kay. You have as many children as you want." She didn't ask Mady's name or come to see her.

Every morning before I close my eyes to go to sleep, I hear my daughters waking, and I think life might be hard for my mother now. I wonder if she's up to her old tricks, wearing a different wig every day. Maybe her neighbors wonder how many women live in her house, but it's only her going through two dresses a day – one for morning and one for evening.

I imagine what her life is like. Everything goes on like a slow clock ticking until the day my father's attorneys find her and she talks to them about me and my daughters as if she has seen us only yesterday.

She might still fool men who see her from far away. She's seventy years old now, but with the wig, the girdle, and the sharp points jutting out of her reinforced, double-padded, under-wire bra, she probably looks like a younger woman from a distance. I also take into account the way she walks – movie star on a dark road enveloped in the headlights of passing cars before her own tragic death on the screen.

I was fifteen years old when I became a candy striper at the old hospital, Memorial. That seems like such a long time ago.

Medicine has changed so much since then. I remember my first patient who had gangrene. I had to help the nurses put live maggots on his leg to clean the dead flesh away. He survived, and his leg healed. But whether or not my patients recovered, I never talked to my mother about what went on in that hospital. She never would have understood why I wanted to be near the sick instead of near her.

Even when I went on to become a nurse's assistant in college, I was still the youngest worker there. The other nurses watched out for me. They told me how many pots of coffee to drink to make it through the night shift and how to talk to men before I bathed them in their beds.

"Oh, and another thing," the nurse behind the desk said with a knowing look, "never wash them there."

"I wouldn't be caught dead. . . . I'd die first."

"I know. Honey, I know. But if they ever give you any trouble – they'll give you trouble. They'll try to say they're too tired, they're just too weak, the medications gotten to them, they can't move their arms, they just can't do it. . . . Just shove the cloths into their lying mouths and tell them they will."

There was no place for romance at the hospital where I had to dress men and women with stringy, useless arms like fragile dolls. In the old building, where I walked when my dolls were still in my father's attic and it hadn't even occurred to me to listen to names I would like to give to my daughters, the halls were always bathed in the same yellow lights. The hospital light changed the women who walked through the halls, making red lipstick a vile orange.

When I was in nursing school, I didn't know why I loved working the night shift. Now I know it was the huge, dark hospital windows where I once saw my mother watching me. I saw the highway lights behind her – white, gold, and flickering red.

"Mother," I said. She mouthed that same word back to me.

Her face was really my face, and there was no one standing outside the windows. It had been a long night. I was alone on the inside entrance, and the sick were waiting in the halls behind me.

After my first child was born, that hospital was torn down. It was the last place where I could see my mother in the night windows, wearing the same white slacks, the same white shoes, even after Labor Day. Every time I saw my reflection in the glass, I thought I was becoming her. But I was wrong. I was never like her, and I never met anyone who was.

MY EXHIBIT IN THE BLUE MUSEUM

San Francisco, August 1962. I was walking through the museum. She was with the women near the beach on the edge of the sunlit garden. The window looked out onto the women. I was on the inside. My face was reflected in the beveled glass. I walked through a room of pale fur stained in orange dye. Plastic statues cast long shadows in the teal lights. She said I must wear white so my dress in the light would be the color of the sky. The sky was also the color of my eyes. My skin was pale enough to reflect the fire behind the violet glass. My hands turned jade. I didn't want to live in that light.

Dallas, January 1974. It's just a dream. Don't think about it.

Arizona, November 7, 1949. I am born today. It's raining. There is something wrong with my eyes. They don't open. She's crying. Even though he's far away, the smoke of his old cigars is trapped inside me. I need him to light up close to my face. I need his cigar near my lips so I can inhale the smoke with him. Her blood is still in my mouth. The milk is in my blood. I share it with her.

Treasure Isle Motel, Galveston, Texas, September 1970. He has a face like a baron in an old painting, smirking as he carves faces into the headboard with a rusted knife. Wearing a black lace gown and playing a Spanish guitar all through the night, she's with him. Why did I come here? When I wake in the morning, I forget. She bathes alone before leaving us. For the rest of the day, he watches me. The knife whittles the wood to white chips in the silence.

November 7, 1949. In darkness, I feel her breathing above me. She shakes the cradle, and I feel the ocean rising behind my eyes. The moon pulls the tide away from the shore until my arm is in her hand and someone is screaming. I touch her face to feel her lips opening on my fingers. *What has she done to me?* she says. *What has she done?* What does her face look like? Does it look like mine? Am I a part of her? Will I grow up to be the same woman? What is a woman? Why is she with me? He pulls her away from me, then lifts me high into the air to touch my nose to his nose. His beard is straw. His breath is ashes.

February 1984. Sorrowful laughter all through the night when I see gnats swimming in my glass of red wine and ask her, *Who would want to live in L.A.?*

Amsterdam, April 19, 1979. No one realizes who I am. I came here to forget my dreams. The red-light district is the most beautiful place I have ever known. Brown tulips are woven into my simple hair. The women beckon to me, their hips pressed against the glass. Consuming the cheapest cigarettes I can find, I blow smoke into the night air. She strikes another match for me. The flame flutters. It rises and falls with my breasts. The yellow light hovers near her mouth and warms my hand before she blows the fire out.

Beacon Street, December 1995. Lobster on white plates, red wine in blue-stem glasses, my hair heavy with turquoise beads, I eat alone. My shadow is like a hunched woman on the painted wall. The mural is a seascape, a white motel, angels flying near the windows where lovers caress in the night. The world is like a Chagall stripped of its wonder. It hurts me to see the angels' faces reflected in the black glass. Like twined lovers, they mean nothing to me. They have cats' eyes, foxes' teeth, and no noses. The lobster burns my tongue. Its juices spurt onto my hands as I crack the bright shell, thinking of the animals that have died for me. The flesh is so tender.

Miami, November 7, 1999. Forgive a fifty-year-old woman for smoking a fat cigar. My mouth is bruised. I'm not going to take this isolation, the window looking out onto a crumbling wall. A boy wanted me near the old high school. Tonight I tell him to come inside. He backs me against the stove. I strike his mouth. His cock is nothing like a cheap cigar, but my mouth feels like an ashtray. My face is burning.

Arizona, November 8, 1949. Buses are running through the city. The air outside the window smells like gasoline, rising fumes like currents rippling on the morning gales. She will not feed me. "Get it away from me," she screams. "Richard, get it away." He holds me. I didn't know if his name was Richard.

Miami, June 1992. How do I know what this life means?

Galveston, summer 1970. I will live here, so close to the shore no one can stop me from drowning. The radio plays the same songs from L.A. She doesn't know where I am. He's somewhere searching, maybe on a plane. Maybe he's coming to me by train. Either way, he sees trees and water, rainy sky, and tiny houses in the distance, all outside a square window. He will not find me. I am never in the same square he's in. He doesn't know what he's looking for. And who am I to tell him?

March 7, 1997. I buy a silver lantern from a milk-glass candle store. Stars are cut into the tin roof below the little handle. Spheres are etched into the windows. The glass door unhinges. I start a small fire to smolder inside the glass, ten tiny tealights flickering. A moth flutters to the flames. Night falls. On the dark balcony, all my candles are burning. I lean into the vanilla-scented light. The wind blows the candles out, one by one. White wax clots in my hair.

San Francisco, August 1962. There must be some mistake. I am outside the other window. She's inside. There are blue flowers on the trees where she goes. On the other side of the glass, her mouth is moving. I can't hear what she's saying, but from her cabernet lips I read her words. "Don't look at me," she says.

Arizona, 1950. The room swings back and forth, back and forth, so fast I can't see the window from the walls. She holds me with her arms straight out, so my body will not touch her body. The cradle rocks in the lamplight in the corner, far away. The nightlight burns pink. A plastic whale with glass eyes covers the tulip bulb; the white spray of the ocean under its belly as it leaps above the waves, close to the violet moon. The mobile above the crib is a glow-in-the-dark galaxy recharged by sunlight and lamplight. In the darkness, it shines above me, always just out of reach. Mars collides with Venus, tangling the strings. They will never untangle, no matter how she tries. She'll have to cut them apart after she cuts my hair. Jupiter spins above me, hypnotizing me with its delicate motions.

Ithaca, New York, June 2001. How do I know what happened? The bodies were exhumed from their graves, seven times, at my request. The county coroner keeps digging up the coffins with the city's yellow machines. I think he hates me. His green eyes are full of distinct imperfections like precious stones. I could identify his irises by their flaws alone. Maybe he is the only man I have ever truly loved. The headstone is white marble, gray-veined. Beneath the carved Mary, the words read, IN LOVING MEMORY – JANE DARRLING, RICHARD DARRLING – JAN. 16,1929 – MARCH 17, 1997; APRIL 21, 1920 – MARCH 17, 1997. *Now we see a dim reflection as in a mirror. Then we shall see each other face to face.*

Arizona, November 6, 1949. The voices sound far away, although no one knows I can hear them. In darkness, I feel I am a part of her. I am her. She is me. Because we are two parts of the same woman, she hates me as she hates herself. My eyes won't open. What are eyes? I see her thoughts as she sees them. I hear the voice inside competing with the voices outside. I remember places I will never know, faces long lost to her. There is a day inside her where her mother has never been born, a year when her grandfather's skin turns to ashes. What is a mother? What is born? There is an alligator gliding through a green river, a blue shell in a black hand.

Green River, June 1955. In this inner tube, my body floats really slowly. Next time, I'll bring my dog Dixie and hold on to her. Like a water balloon, my stomach is heavy, but I float without sinking. The artificial beach behind the plantation house is full of white sand under a crypt of gray water. I spy on the travelers photographing the statues in the mimosa garden. We have no waves. There are no rapids. Waves are like wind; they carry the dirt away. I could take the white water rapids to another delta, but there are no other deltas, and all the statues are of dead men and their horses. In the garden, behind the gates, the women's eyes are like her eyes, watering, blinking, sad because of the undershadows.

Los Angeles, September 1986. Tight jeans, black jacket, I'm in the back of a limousine, speeding fast away. A woman with a hand-twisted silver belt ties her chain to mine. Her lips are on my lips, then she's sucking the red powder off my face. The traffic slows down. We come to a full stop on the freeway. People are honking at one another, throwing lit cigarettes out the windows. There is a fire burning near the highway, chemical smoke rising in the distance. The smoke becomes part of the sky, just another type of cloud blocking the sun. The woman's red hair is long with perfect stiff curls that spring back to their coils whenever I try to pull them straight. "Baby, don't do that," she says. "What are you doing? Stop." Then her hand is unzipping my jeans and her fingers are inside me. Then my hand is on her hand, pulling back. Her small breasts are in my face, smothering me, smelling of talcum powder and aloe lotion. "Suck it," she says, and I do.

Galveston, 1979. This child, this child, it keeps calling me home. There is no home, I tell it. Where did it come from? Where will it go? Anywhere but here. Away from me, some place where children go, the summer nights in the green lots behind the hotels where the small arms hold each other underground. No one knows I left them there.

Enid, Oklahoma, 1980. This is flat country, wide open, with plains and plains of farmland. The lightning here takes up the whole sky. Whenever a storm hovers over the evening, I am here. I walk the shoulder during the day, venturing out into the fields. I trespass, hopping the barbed wire into the prairie, into the wheat, into the distance. I go where the cows go, crossing the cattle guard, onto the white road to the highway. Stumbling into midnight traffic, I am stunned by headlights, waiting for the right vehicle to run me down.

Houston, April 1980. I walked the dark streets, hoping to find a way home.

March 18, 1997. I take her hands into my hands. We are alone. I don't know who she is, so how could she know me? Her dress is made of glitter, fake jewels on metal strings sewn to the sheer fabric, hanging like a beaded fringe. The dress is heavy, and I know she feels the weight as she walks, the small, cut glass flitting in the moonlight. Then the fake diamonds are everywhere, scattering over the street. They bounce on the pavement, falling like rain. "Help me," she says, and I kneel down to pick up the pieces one by one before dropping them into her hand. Later, the dress is hanging on my bedroom door, and she's in the tub with the bathroom door open. The phone rings, and the policewoman says there's been a homicide. There wasn't a scratch on them, and no one knows the cause of death. Her eyes were open, and the house was in order. She died in his arms, but he died before she died. The woman in the tub looks at me, her hair white with shampoo. Her leg dangles over the edge, her wet foot dripping onto the floor. She closes her eyes and puts her head underwater. "Breathe," I tell her, but she doesn't hear me.

San Francisco, August 1962. There are girls here who look like me, long blond hair and ice-blue eyes. Behind the glass, sad music plays on a scratched piano. "Dance," he says, and all the girls begin to sway. "Sing," he says, and they mouth the words to a distant lullaby. People pay to see us. We are part of the museum. I am the last major exhibit. For an extra fee, the visitors are allowed to go behind the glass and ask me questions. They are allowed to touch my hair and hold my hands. "Were you always this way?" some ask. "Do you live here? Why are your eyes like that? How do you know the others? Are you all related? What happens when the exhibit closes for the night? What do you eat? How did you get your hair so straight?" I just keep singing, pretending I don't understand their words.

Galveston, October 1976. The baby can't speak, but it understands me somehow. I tell it I am not its real mother. I say I will have to go away and that its real mother will find it after I've gone. If I say good-bye, it starts to cry. If I say hello, it tries to stick its foot in its mouth. I don't want to touch it, but someone has to touch it. Someone has to pick it up and hold it and dip it in a bucket of water. Someone has to put a hand over its mouth to bring back the silence.

Abandoned beach house, August 1991. The water seeped inside, lapping at the walls. The floor fell through, the boards warping, moldering, fading under my feet. The gray water smells of white fish dying. A crab drifts across the stair. A seahorse is trapped in the small closet. I let the hammerhead out. I went deeper inside. I opened the other door. Diving down, I walked on my hands, touching the holes in the boards, the place where the floor used to be. There are old photographs on the walls. They crumbled in the dampness, but I can see his face, so thin he's grim. I love him, and yet he's a stranger to me still. How could I say what he is like? There's a woman walking outside the house, a trespasser like me.

It's easier to describe her face as she watches me through the window. I could follow her across the shale in the evening and know her better than I ever knew him. I could touch her face, if she let me, and remember its contours for the rest of my life.

Hollywood Blvd., November 20, 1987. She's clever enough not to frighten me as long as she wants to have me around. I follow her like a pet poodle through the streets. She's not as humble or naïve as I was led to believe by her silence. She leads me into darker alleys. Maybe she's too modest or too nervous to reach behind her to stroke my hair. There's a big hole in her handbag where her gun shows through. I don't think there's any warning I can see as she walks from corner to corner, looking for open doors. Her gun is made of black candy that tastes like cinnamon, and she lets me taste it, putting the gun in my mouth. It can't hurt anyone, but it horrifies people, so she waves it through the night.

New Orleans, September 1996. I watched my scratched face in the mirror for a long time, smiling at myself, trying to remember who I was and where the scratches came from as I dipped the brush into the orange gloss.

Arizona, June 1950. Sunflowers bloom outside the window. Their dark faces sway in the wind, and I want to be one of them. I want to crawl outside the house and live outside the window looking in. I don't know how the sunflowers speak to one another, bees traveling the leaves, seeds falling to dust, pollen on the wind. I don't know if they have eyes. But if they see, they see this girl on the other side of the window, the one I've seen in the mirrors with a crusted face. There's something wrong with her eyes. When she wakes in the morning, they won't open. She thinks she's blind. Her world is full of darkness. The woman holds her still, leaning on her legs. The man wipes her face with the warm cloth. Then he uses the scalpel to retrace the slits in her eyes so they will open on their own. Then she can see again. She is me. I am her. The man and the woman are crying. I see their faces in the morning light from the window. By evening, the girl begins to heal again, and the slits close for good, scabbing over so her eyes won't open. She hears crying and running water. He picks her up. She leans her face into the steam, and it helps me somehow.

Galveston, spring, 1972. At night, the hotel lights shine gold on gray water. He blows smoke into my hair, and I share the cigarette with him. "Babe," he says, "you have the bluest eyes in the world. I've never seen anyone like you. You're so perfect. Do you know how beautiful you are?" I look at him as if for the last time, trying to memorize the delicate lines at the corners of his eyes and his sincere expression. This is what I want to remember, that he thinks I have beautiful eyes. The shore glimmers silvery in the moonlight. We swim in the dark ocean. The water is as warm as my blood on his hands the night he leaps from the balcony with the baby in his arms.

Oklahoma City, October 1995. I dream I'm on a white cruise ship sailing a blue ocean to a distant land, my shadow rippling on the wind-struck sails.

Arizona, November 7, 1949. The nurses take me away from her legs and put me in a glass box. A camera flashes, blinding me with its light. It's the light of my life, burning so bright I see blue in the darkness behind my eyelids. They won't open the glass. The flashes dissolve into one another. The light flares away too soon. I want to touch the people's faces. Instead, I touch the glass. When she holds me, I see with my mouth as it opens on her breast. I see with my tongue and my hands. I see with my ears as she cries. Water washes over me like his forgiveness.

Galveston, February 1972. I drank a bottle of wine on the beach and started laughing but couldn't stop, even though nothing seemed funny anymore.

Arizona, May 3, 1965. A big black fish in the green aquarium with plastic seaweed swims toward my fingers pressed against the glass. Lovebirds fight in the pastel cage overhead. Their wings look like a cream feather shawl brushed in rouge powder. They fight in chatter, fluttering into the bars as the long-haired cat circles below. I chew pink gum and relish the corn syrup, pressing my lips to the aquarium to blow the fish a kiss. The fish swims away from my eyes. The aerator is fast and good. In the clean water, bubbles rise through sunlight. Outside the window, the other children are rejoicing. The lovebirds coo above my face reflected like a stranger's in the gleaming glass. I feel like a switchboard operator every time the phone rings. I say, "Hello." The voices say, "How can I reach her?" She is far away. No man can touch her unless she runs to him like a little girl making her way through a crowded street in the night. She's a careful traveler, a sly fish swimming through dark water.

Arizona, December 1959. The gates slam behind me, and the dogs bark. As if I've come to the wrong house, she refuses to unlock the door and let me come inside.

Amsterdam, 1979. The women were so beautiful I wanted to be one of them. I wanted to call them sister, lover, friend. Instead, I had to call them whore and pay to touch them. I had to pay extra for them to look inside my open legs and tell me what they saw there. They stroked me as they talked so I would listen to what they whispered in the rose light. And how could I say to them, *I know you, I am you, although I have never seen you before and will never see you again unless I pay and pay until all my money is gone.* And I began to pray, my voice echoing near the Old Church. *I am nothing. I am no one.* No one asked my name. No one wanted to hear it, to remember what I'd done in what some say is a lewd city. I say it is the only place I could ever always find arms to hold me, where I could see my face in every window whether or not my vacant eyes were reflected in the glass. *I love you, I love you,* I said, my voice beginning to break as it trailed off into the smoky silence. *What's it going to be?* another woman asked, her eyes looking into mine as if she wished I were a man. She winced as I put my hands on her shoulders. *What are you doing?* she whispered into my hair. *This wasn't part of the deal.* There wasn't enough money in the world that night for her to look at me steadily as if I was what she wanted. I was gone before she could feel the shock of my hand touching her hand under the black curtain.

L.A., December 1999. The coat looks like a lion's mane, soft and yellow and tattered, gleaming like a dog in the sun. The fur is so fake that if I touch the tip of my cigar to the ratted hairs the coat will melt like doll's hair. Like a clown's wig on fire, it will go up in a single flare without a long flame and turn to black liquid on my arms and legs. Then I would be naked and alone, standing near the street at rush hour, my skin burning, dripping black liquid onto the pavement.

L.A., October 1989. I dream this sad dream and then the city goes away like light on a woman's arms as she passes under a dark tunnel. The traffic moves too fast before it slows down for no reason. I feel the breeze on the backs of my knees, my hair so long it tickles my wrists as I walk the street at night, turning to remember where I'm going. Smoke streams out of a woman's mouth. I move like that, a lit cigarette passed from one stranger to another before it burns too short and a woman tosses it into a barrel of fire.

Arizona, 1953. In the bath water, the bubbles burst, and her hand is like a big gray fish swimming through my hair.

New Orleans, April 1963. The wedding in the abandoned chapel begins in a stream of aqua-tinted water draining from a hotel pool alley to the center aisle. The woman reads the vows above her pale reflection in the murky water. *This is the beginning, not the end, although some of us are dying. Some of us can live a lifetime in a day. Some die a thousand deaths but live forever in our minds. The walls are charred by old flames long vanquished, the arsonists' hands grown cold.* The carved benches are nailed to the floor, the walls marred by knives and faded graffiti. The chapel was vandalized summer after summer until the congregation boarded the doors and moved to another side of the city. Teenagers pried the doors off their hinges, tearing down the chains, receiving a never-ending flow of drifters so children could pray in the night beneath the statue of the virgin with no nose. The woman strikes a match, lighting a candle. Sparks hiss into the water. Her voice rises above me, echoing off the glass dome. Her song is the evening bird's call that lets in the night. Her hips sway to the music of an acoustic guitar. Her steady hands hold the damp paper. Her skin is too white. It hurts my eyes to see her legs in the candle's glare. The orange light plays like sunlight through her fingers. I see her bright eyes focused on me. Her song is so high it makes the broken chandeliers chime. People put their hands over their ears, and I'm crying. Hers is the song I hear for the rest of my life. Her voice will not fade. Her sound will not go away, even though this is the first and the last time I will hear it. My ears pop, as if something is breaking inside my head. I look into the red and gold stained-glass windows. Later, alone in my bed, I pick a crust of dried blood from my ears.

Galveston, 1973. Smile, he says. *You're on stage.*

New York City, 1980. These are the best items I've stolen: a purple tiara, a silver leopard, a glass bell, and a ring with a clear stone that changes colors when hands touch it in the dark.

Arizona, October 1950. Her fingers massage my eyes, forcing the slits apart. The butterfly ring grazes my forehead. A bell rings, clanging on a chain outside my window. Red leaves whirl in the wind. "Close the window," she says. "Richard, draw the curtains. It's cold. Someone might see us." A shadow falls across the hall, darkening the doorway. The lights go down. They were all I could ever really see – lights, shadows, movement – until he held my eyelids open and his face was in my face, eclipsing the lamplight, his eyes the first blue I would ever see. *What is blue?* I wanted to ask him. The ocean was in his eyes. *What are eyes?* A shuddering above me, his lashes brushed my cheeks. "Baby," he says, "baby, it's all right." The lamp falls from the table, smashing into the wall, swinging from the cord, making a circle of light that travels over the floor. *What is light?* Through a slit in the curtains, the red leaves fall and I want to hold them. I want to bring them into the room with me until the darkness takes them away.

L.A., 1981. The evening sky is pink-hued above the wires in the wind, trembling outside the window. The dream becomes a vision of my father. The wires tangle above the skylight as the storm comes. As the sun goes down, the shadows move slowly across the bed, the shadow of the wires etched across my legs. My jeans are tossed aside, crumpled in a heap on the burgundy carpet. The fogged mirror is silvered with my prints as I have touched it to steady myself against the pain. The prints darken the glass, then turn black against the amber lights. The nail holes lengthen, and the nails begin to pull through, as I hold the frame too long. The white candle melts into a gray pool. The wax hardens as it cools, losing its translucence. I see the flame in the mirror, rising and falling with the man's breath. I move my hips like the flame, light turning ash to dust as the wick burns short. I am giving my pain away. He is giving it back to me. This is no way for enlightened people to get along, to push a woman against a wall, to hold onto a mirror with sticky hands, gazing at a terrible face and thinking it's beautiful. He lays me down. The wires above me twist apart as the birds fly away. The shadows dissect my body in the fading light. He will not trace the shadows with his hands, so I trace them for him. He will not leave, so I tell him to go away. His lips on my ear, he whispers, "Fuck this," and his breath is like smoke rising from the fire that burns my hair.

Arizona, October 1953. Listen. The wind whistles like a train through the cracks in the walls. The wind makes music, tangling the chimes. The chimes clang like bells on the breeze as it rises, shaking the treetops. The oil smoke comes like a putrid stream drifting from the kitchen where catfish fry. The bones are scattered under the window in the flowerbed near the triangular heads with tiny eyes. He cleans the fish with a knife, shearing the fins, the silver gleaming like blood as he removes the bones from the flesh.

San Francisco, September 2001. It's kind of like this dream I've always had – she's there and she's not there, then she slaps me across the face and one of my teeth falls to the tile, clicking against the grating as it slips through the air vents.

Tulsa, 1997. I lied to a man with dark hair because he had a kind mouth. He asked if I was from Oklahoma. I said I had been there all my life, moving from one old house to another like a simple hostage, a growing snake casting off its old skin. In his car at night, I am vulnerable as a rattler recently shed. Flinching as he touches me, I close my eyes. His hand moves up my skirt, exploring in silence as we drive up the rickety bridge. I don't know where we're going, and I don't want to know how this night will end, his sleepy face in the orange light as he pulls my hair and the strands stick to his mouth as he brushes me away. Outside his car, the traffic stream slows. When he waves, I walk a highway I don't know. My head hurts so badly behind my eyes I think my skull is shrinking.

Amsterdam, 1979. In crowds, I walk with a woman through the darkness to the bar lights, laughing at a joke I don't understand because I have friends now, even though I don't know their real names. Behind the glass doors, the women are like the lovers I never had, damaged, displayed, gazing out at strangers in the night as they comb their hair in violet light. A brunette beckons to me, tapping on the glass. Together we could put the damn in Amsterdam, but I can't afford to hold her tonight. Men's harsh voices crow all through the dark. Teenagers bathe in the canal.

Women untangle their hair in boredom after throwing glasses of water into men's faces. This isn't the way I thought the city would be. I wasn't ready for this shame, this lonely hour when I have nowhere to go, when the woman struts away from me, holding a pilot's dark hand, waving good-bye. Her face turns away from his flinty eyes. My hands smell like sweat, fallen leaves, crumpled bills, and old coins growing warm in my hip pocket. I walk through the glass door. The other woman's eyes are like the green of a delicate wineglass I left behind, the stem so fragile I snapped it without thinking. *What are you doing here?* she asks. I don't know. *How did you find me?* I came out of the night, into the darkness. I didn't know where I was going. I didn't realize that it was almost morning. A new day was beginning. I just opened the door and walked inside, and she was looking at me as if she didn't know what to do. So she took my face into her large, soft hands and I started to laugh, although I couldn't remember why I was shivering near her.

Oklahoma, 1955. My great-great grandmother was attacked by mad hogs.

March 17, 1997. Where has she gone? Someone says, "To hell and back." The traffic light changes from green to yellow, but the yellow is as dim as her jaundiced eyes and the green looks as blue as the ocean photograph. She has the face of the ivory Madonna with no arms, so still and so colorless in the white light. I sigh, reaching my hand to her nose to see if I can feel her breathing. She is human, but she isn't like me. On the television, the doctor says all babies are born with blue eyes and the eyes change color over time. But what is blue, to be the first color? And for that matter, what is color, to be constantly changing? What good are eyes if color changes and what good are babies if we can only see them for what they are, never what they will be? *I can't go on*, I write in my last note to her, hoping she will save it, unfolding the crumpled paper again and again for the world to see, like the dim photographs of me in the places I could never remember with the women I would never really know. Paris, in the dark hotel, the smoke clinging to my hair in pale morning light. The blue distance over the fields in Oklahoma, the largest sky I've ever seen. The canal houses in Amsterdam, the doors opening and closing like mouths in the night. The beautiful evening when the sky turned pink before a storm in L.A. and I fell to my knees, my arms reaching out to a new moon I could barely see.

Arizona, October 2, 1956. "Quit dragging the old photos out into the light," she whispers.

San Francisco, December 25, 1960. In the study, I discover twenty-year-old irises pressed into the *World Book Encyclopedia E*. The old petals turn the pages black, and the flowers fall apart as I pull them away from the paper. Then I see the imprints of the letters on the brittle stems.

L.A., June 1962. Like a painter of peasant life, I imagine farmers praying near their wives in the plowed fields. But there are no fields near me tonight, although there are more barrels of food and starving children in my dreams than the farmers would ever see. In the morning, I chase the green flies out of the house. I walk naked to the dark trees, pinching my breasts in boredom because I want to force my body to feel something, even if it's only pain. The old house falls to ruins, the violet walls crumbling like broken skin inside the historic masonry. I slept behind the white curtains. I woke with the light streaming through. A man was standing in my balcony window. I would not let him touch me, but he held my wrist anyway. Taking hold of my arms, he had control of me. Where was I to go? The house was my house. In a perfect world, I was supposed to be the only one inside.

Arizona, April 7, 1954. When he hangs the high light, *Higher,* she says, *no, to the left.* And he drills holes into the ceiling, the white dust falling onto our faces.

Miami, January 2001. Why do I want this? You tell me. I was never the smart one, always trying to say what I meant, but never quite meaning what I said. Always trying to say what I felt, but never able to put the feeling into words. Is it any wonder I'm still alone? Is it any wonder no one understands me? That no man has ever touched my hair without backing me into some corner of a room where I didn't ask to go? In dreams, I see another woman's face in place of my own. Her eyes are not my eyes. They are brown, not blue. Blue is the only color I could never get away from, that and the yellow of my hair as the sun goes down. I will never look into a mirror again, but I'll always know what I look like. There are women like me all over the busy streets, bleaching their hair at nightfall so they will stand out in the crowds before they grow too old to desire.

Houston, 1999. Hey, I say to the other hitchhiker, *you're a liar, but at least you're still alive.*

Arizona, 1957. She is the one I thought would never go away. I found a photo of her, the purple scar zigzagging across her left breast like a streak of lightning across the morning sky. In the next shot, the milk streams from her, following the scar's trail to my open mouth. My lips cover the tip of the scar without understanding the old wound. I will never know what it means although I will carry its taste in my mouth for the rest of my life. The television blares above the radio, and her voice rises above the static-injected music. Her humming calms me down. He is in the songs, traveling farther away, his deep voice trapped inside the gospel music. Sometimes I am sorry that he sang to us, although I never understood what his songs meant or why he kept leaving us behind. The garage was his house before he burned it down. The water heater was a ball of fire when she carried me through the blazing walls. The heat singed my eyelids apart so that when my eyes opened all I saw was her sweet face in the firelight.

San Francisco, August 16, 1963. "You're forgiven," he says. And then I'm quiet.

L.A., 1984. Near my favorite bar, a man plays guitar outside the heavy door where women's names are etched into the blue paint.

LAUREL is scrawled just above my eyes. Inside, ants crawl through the kitchen and a woman with long dark hair buys me a greenish drink that tastes like sour apples. The drink makes me happy, so I dance with her, my boots clomping on the wood floor. A black ant crawls on her hair. She flicks it away, into a stranger's drink. A man rises, hitting his head on the chain lamp, and the light flutters. "Come here," he says. I feel the heft of his belly pressing against my back as she slips her tongue into my ear.

March 17, 1997. She died today. She died! I screamed to no one. And then he died. But no, that's not what really happened, not what I was told. He died on the big bed, his back resting against the white wall, his empty palms tilted up to the ceiling where the heavens were painted in a gaudy mural. Then she crawled gently into his lap, her long peach dress covering his hands. She put her face to his face as she took her last breath. It took an hour for her to let go. She sat on his body all that time, waiting as the foam streamed out of his mouth. The foam means chaos. They drank it together. *After all that's happened, we still love each other,* she wrote. *And no one can take that away.* But what type of poison was it? And did he know he would die also? And did she ever think of me? What was the last thing that happened?

Amsterdam, 1979. At the coffee shop, she helps me choose some nice leaves that are said to bring luster to dingy skin and to make dull hair shine bright in the sun. We share the joint filled with medicinal herbs on the way to our hotel, but she won't really let me smoke it. Even though it smells like old feet, she keeps hogging the whole thing, saying it's probably poison and telling me not to inhale under the balcony covered in yellow and blue tulips. At night, she leaves me behind. Slipping past the gates, I see the tulips in the moonlight and wonder why I ever left. Women sit on the pink benches, smoking cigarettes near the bus stops. I wave to a girl with short red hair, knotted into tight braids and heavy with jade beads. "Fine," she says, "fine," shaking her hair and blowing smoke into my face as she rises. Grabbing my small wrist in her ring-jeweled hand, she leads me past the terraces to a narrow room shaped like a walk-in closet. On the lime walls, shiny X rays of a skull with dark spots inside like bad CAT scans cover the bricked-in windows. "What are these?" I ask, thinking they are some type of new art until her green eyes begin to water. "My mom," she whispers. I empty my pockets, dumping all my cash on her table. She walks to the record player and turns on ballet music. Stretching her legs against the walls, she contorts until her knee is in her hand and her foot is behind her head.

Arizona, 1950. Hush, baby, baby, she sings long before I know how to talk to her. *Don't say a word.*

New Orleans, 1981. I watched her touch the stone angel's eyes. She fell to her knees in the graveyard, and he covered her shoulders in black shawls, the moonlight through the lace casting strange shadows over her pale hair. Although it begins to rain, she refuses to leave, and he has to stay with her, so I linger near the trees, the leaves some small shelter against the damp air. The small pond I look into reflects a lovely face, still as a porcelain mask I don't recognize as my own. My tears fall into the water and mingle with the dying rain. Whimpering like a child that night, I remembered my still body aching in the old brick hotel where I stripped near strangers on the black-iron balcony and entered the red room through warped doors. My shadow was long on the crimson walls. I walked through a room of violin music and the song never stopped for me. The players only had eyes for their instruments gleaming in the candlelight.

San Francisco, 1963. The museum is full of elegant statues, chiseled to perfection, the stone faces cold to the touch. The angels kneel to yellow flames. The magician stretches her wings under the blue star. The empress stands near the emperor, his face obscured by the robe's hood. With the other girls, I have to ring sopping rags of soapy water and clean the statues' faces and hands. He watches from the bayside garden. She stands near the tower, below the space where the moon will rise in the evening. At night, we will hold hands, walk to the shore, and take turns bathing one another's hair in the dark water. Cleanliness and peaceful chores before dancing and deep sleep, she taught us that much. In the mornings, people will pay to watch her brush our hair and ask her how fast it grows.

Amsterdam, 1979. Behind pink windows, my hands are pressed against the glass. A curtain rises before it falls. Inside, she makes me dance with another woman even though I don't want to dance and I don't know why we're dancing. The stage is set in a circle of gold lights beaming as if ready to ignite under gas flame. He takes green tickets at the door until his coat pockets are bulging and someone helps him light a new cigar. When the doors open, I hear church bells ringing in the distance and wonder if it's still night. I only want to go backstage and fall asleep in the makeshift bed. But the stagelights are turning colors from yellow to rose to violet tinged with green. The men are crying out for more, tossing money at my feet. The stagelights make faces strange, reflecting off teeth and making huge circles under eyes. The men raise their glasses to me. I bow again and again before the night is over, even though the sun rose hours ago.

Galveston, June 1973. Once the riptide carried me away. He pulled me back to shore and started breathing his breath into my mouth.

San Francisco, 1980. I go back to the museum for the first time in more than ten years. But I can't find it. No one I've told believes what happened, especially since I can't find the old building. Someone besides me has to remember it. She says, *It's a dream.* He says, *It's a lie.* On the other side of the city, I found remnants of the broken statues in a gated junkyard. The rest showed up in newspaper photos before the police auction. She always told me never to believe the news. "Close your eyes," he said before setting the pages on fire. At the crowded auction, he tried to buy the statues back but was outbid every time. Feeling sorry for him, I put my hands on his hands, stroking the curly dark hairs before he turned away.

Arizona, November 7, 1949. Through the grasses, she walks toward the sunlight and the weeds to the shadow in the distance. Carrying me, her face close to mine, she shakes me with her steps. I feel her breath on my mouth. *Please,* she whispers, *let this be the last time.* I wrap my hands around her hair. She tries to unwind the strands from my fingers, forcing my hands apart, but I keep winding back. The wind picks up speed. Her shoulder smells like dandelion lotion. I put her necklace in my mouth, sucking on the cross.

Texas, 1993. The tires on the dirt road kick up gravel on the way to the green fields where black horses graze. I drink hot coffee from the metal thermos. The man with the white hat stops the pickup, gets out, and waves his gun around. He unlocks the gate. The rusted metal sighs on its hinges, and the horses stand still, watching us. He points the gun at the sky and fires at the clouds. I get down on my hands and knees and begin to crawl through the young trees and yellow flowers. In my woven bag, I gather white stones and cattle bones as a dark horse leans down to sniff my hair.

San Francisco, December 1961. Hey, I say, *come here.* "Hey what?" *Hey, you.* "No," he says, "hey, Daddy."

Amsterdam, 1979. In the hundred-year-old theater, she holds my wrist and says, "I would like to remind you they are not always women." We walk though the beautiful blue rooms, examining perfume bottles and ivory figurines before the show begins. Her face in the lamplight looks tired. The lines around her mouth have grown deeper, and she is getting new wrinkles under her eyes. Staring at her, I pull her closer to the light that makes the shadows under her wrinkles darker. When she first began to look old, I was angry with her, wondering why she never discussed these changes with me or asked my permission. She had always been the strong one, but I realize I have grown stronger. It will be this way for the rest of our lives. The stage music begins to play, the drum beat throbbing behind the painted walls, making the picture frames shudder.

Arizona, April 10, 1950. My dreams are full of white diamonds that fall into the river. I wake to his breath on my ear. He stands over the cradle. His beard brushing my eyelids, he strikes a match against the cradle bars. I smell the smoke again as he lights his cigar, and suddenly I'm free. *Open the window*, she says, *you're smothering her.* But he keeps the window closed as if he knows I don't want the fresh air to blow inside. I want to smell his smoke lingering behind him, trapped in the blankets. He holds me, blowing the smoke away from my eyes. I try to take the cigar out of his mouth, but his lips hold it tight. *Look, Linda*, he says, *she's laughing.*

March 17, 1997. In the airport bathroom, the black tiles are cold against my cheek and suddenly I'm sure she has died. A woman in a yellow dress looks into the big mirror. Brushing the charcoal powder around her eyes, she sees me in the reflection and drops her compact onto the floor. The tiny mirror shatters. She walks slowly toward me and leans down, the shadow of her hair falling across my face. *I believe you*, she says. *I believe you for the first time.* She reaches into her leather purse, rummaging through the lipsticks in their navy cases and the silvery pens. After taking out a red envelope, she hands it to me. *Open it*, she says. *It's a photo of your face as a young girl.* In the photograph, the purple scars around my eyes are just beginning to fade. My irises are as blue as the June sky above me. The woman helps me stand. Together we walk out of the terminal into the rain, sheltered under her white umbrella.

Miami, 1999. The boy kisses me with his eyes closed. I kiss him back. He's so drunk on lemon rum he's too sick to stand, so I cradle him in my arms on the floor littered with newspapers and struck matches. Lighting a raspberry candle, I raise his face to the flame that flickers near his lips so full I have to trace them with my fingers. *Help me*, he says, but he's dreaming. For all I know, he doesn't even realize I'm here now or that he's in my room, a thin sheet drenched in sweat and patterned roses wrapped around his narrow waist. I count the hairs on his chest, realizing he is too young to be my son. There are seven hairs in all – three around his left nipple, four around his right. As day breaks, I bathe his face in warm water and wonder what he's thinking. As he opens his eyes, gold blossoms sway on the tree outside the window.

San Francisco, October 1963. The beige bra strap cuts into my shoulder. My sundress is spattered, stained in old blood that is not my own. When I found it crumpled in an orange heap under the stairs and wondered what it was, I told myself it was dog's blood. After washing the dress in the metal sink and hanging it in the window to dry in the sun, I decided to wear it because it was the best I had and maybe nobody would notice the specks. I bought grapes at the fruit stand where a woman with a black eye grabbed my arm and pulled me into the roof's shadow. "Where did you get that dress?" she asked, her breath smelling like old salmon. "It doesn't belong to Mica," she hissed. "It's mine."

Arizona, January 18, 1952. The doctor removes the patch from my right eye and then rips the tape off. I see his face in the dim light and realize he's smiling at me. The nurse pricks my heel with a tiny needle, but my foot won't bleed, so she moves to my fingers. Using narrow tubes to draw the blood, she holds my palm. Afterwards, I touch her wrist, and she starts to cry. *Why is she so quiet?* she says. *Doesn't she see me? She knows we're here.*

L.A., 1984. Fuck me, she says to him, *just fuck me.* And then the house lights are so bright they burn my eyes.

Dallas, 1990. At night in the city, I set a church on fire and a crowd gathers as it burns to the ground near the fire trucks. The people's faces in the dark seem so innocent as the flames light their sorrowful expressions and the smoke blows across the street. One woman begins to sing an old song, and then everyone is singing, even me, although I don't know the words. The next day I see my face in the crowd on the morning news. I stand out in the dark because of my pale hair and my eyes that seem too blue in the firelight. I keep turning channels, waiting for the replay so I can watch my tears fall as the roof falls, but I never wonder what it means.

San Francisco, February 1962. This is the night when none of the other girls will have mercy on me, when she tries to read my horoscope but the signs don't make sense, so she tells me to shuffle the tarot cards. From the new deck, I choose the moon and the stars, the sun and the hanged man, the fool and the tower. At first, she tries to tell me these are good signs, even though some of the cards are facing the wrong way. But he sighs the smoke into her face as he reaches for the hanged man and the tower. He says I will be sacrificed again and again like him and that we are so much alike it hurts him even to look at me. So he turns away, walking out the empty gallery. *He's a liar,* she whispers, as we walk through the dark museum. *But I love him more than you will ever know.* In the white room with the barred windows, she tucks me into bed with the other girls whose coughs rasp through the night. After she turns off the lights, someone calls to her, but she won't come. Our dresses rustle on the rod across the room as if she is counting the garments in their plastic bags. *She can't keep us here forever,* someone says, but she doesn't answer.

Galveston, 1975. Just when the hotel lights go down, the sun comes up gold across the steely water. There's sand in my shoes and itchy grains trapped under my breasts. Rising from the rumpled bed, I smell the salty water on the sheets and begin to realize there are other people in the room, waking with me. A woman with red hair steps out onto the balcony, her bare hips alabaster in the morning light. A man with a long beard and green eyes lights a cigarette and puts it in my mouth before offering me a glass of water. The water tastes strange on my swollen tongue. The drops trickle off my parched lips as if in my new thirst I have somehow forgotten how to swallow.

Oakland, 1986. I was sick for days, but now I'm well. A skinny dog slept on my coat while I dozed beside the green pool, my face burning in the sun, fleas biting my arms. The dog ran away three times but kept coming back, bringing strangers' shoes – strappy black high heels, red boots, and white sneakers. The stolen shoes lay in a heap near my bare feet. The dog rested its face on my chest and looked into my eyes as if waiting for me to repay the gift. I bought a hamburger and fed the greasy meat to him while he whined, licking the slobber from his jaws. I watched him walk away with the last bit of bread in his mouth and knew he was hungry.

Arizona, 1951. Even as a child, I was nocturnal, more like a cat than a girl. I moved silently and could see so well in the dark. She called me an animal, and I rubbed my face against her legs.

San Francisco, November 1963. That night she reaches her hand through the glass-bead curtain and grabs my arm to pull me inside the smoky room where he plays piano. There's metal under my heels, and I'm supposed to tap my shoes in time to his music until the other girls walk through the curtain. A woman will die where she falls at the foot of the stairs behind the museum after it closes. In the audience hours before, she waves to me and smiles at my father dropping bills into the glass bowl before she enters the outer gallery. Time is running out for her as she looks at the ocean paintings, her long fingers playing through my hair. At dinner, I hear a scream outside the kitchen, but I keep eating my spaghetti. Always, I tried to suck the pasta down fast so I might have a little more than the others. But the bowl was empty before I could ask for more.

Dallas, 1975. I fainted at his feet after one glass of the good wine.

March 18, 1997. The searchlights look green above the highway as they filter through the bridge cables. I watch the round light dart across the dark water. I drive past the old house just to see the tape tangled across the front door. There is a yellow light inside and the white flash of cameras as strangers walk through the rooms. I want to see the photographs they've taken, just to see what that night was like. But I know if I ask, my request would mean more suspicion. I'm afraid to talk, afraid to say too much. I know I will keep driving past this house for the rest of my life, but I will never understand what happened inside.

Oklahoma, December 1996. From far away, the branches of the dark trees this winter look like veins bleeding into the white sky.

L.A., 1983. Tea lights illuminated the front door, and the windows stayed open. She was the dark figure standing inside, her long silhouette sleek in the lamplight. She waved me on. I stepped inside. The lamp was behind her hair, obscuring her face, making her curls sparkle like her gold jewelry. The bracelets clanged together, moving up and down her arm as she lifted the wineglass to her mouth and I toasted her health again and again as he crushed his cigar into her scarf.

March 20, 1997. I wanted to make a plaster cast of her face after she died, but people just don't do that anymore. In the jewelry store, I tried on an intricate sapphire necklace and felt the weight of it pulling me down to the counter, all along realizing the necklace was worth more than I was.

Amsterdam, 1979. This was one of the last days that she would be considered beautiful. After that, people would look at her and see only this skinny woman who had stiff hair and wore too much red makeup. Her eyes would no longer be as startling because of the thick glasses. Walking past the picture windows, I saw our reflection – me, the younger woman with white-blond hair down to my ankles and her, the fragile one dressed conservatively in a black pantsuit and looking too uptight to be walking through a street filled with music. After a drink in the pub, we walked through one of the private houses, and she left me behind. As she walked away, her heels clicking on the metal stairs, I could still hear her dusky voice in my ear, *Why don't you just do it? There's a room. It's what you've wanted.* She knew what would happen to me in that house. In the mornings, she came back, but I was often too sore to move. The money was never enough. She washed my hair in the gray tub, knowing I was braver than she was.

Galveston, 1985. I saw her broken veins through the fishnet stockings as we devoured the jumbo shrimp on the white platter. Breaking the thermometer, he said, "That's quicksilver! Catch it if you can." The mercury beads began to roll toward the shrimp tails, away from my hands.

Arizona, 1950. He paints the night sky across my ceiling. She stands below the ladder with the bucket in her hands, her arms stained in blue and silver paint. He changes positions with her, and she traces the sun flare. The stars burn above her. I see a black spot on the planet like Jupiter's volcanic moon. She draws the spiral nebula, the Whirlpool Galaxy. For years, I will fall asleep under Libra and the moon's eclipses. The star-birthing region will explode like a great white vein in the nursery decades before the veins will collapse in her arms, years before I will know what vein means. As my eyes begin to close, the lids crusting over, I imagine myself lost in the Great Rift. In darkness, I envision the sky so lovely it doesn't make sense, the way they sacrificed geography for a beauty I could rarely see.

COROLLA

I was a twelve-year-old girl when my sister Wanda turned twenty-one. That would be our last summer together, but I didn't know it yet. Times like these, the night slowly descending beyond the dockside, I think I never knew my sister. No one ever knew her. She was a dark horse in the night, the lone bird that broke the V as the flock struggled to hold together.

In the summers, she and I lived on the coast of North Carolina in a three-story mauve house near the Atlantic Ocean. The rest of the family shared the upper rooms with us. When I wasn't with her, I was trying to avoid Aunt Joan, our parents, or Wanda's boyfriend, Dougy. The old folks didn't bother me much because they didn't know who I was anymore. They didn't remember the day or the year, but they knew the wars they had fought like the broken veins on the backs of their hands.

Now I'm fighting my own veins as they begin to rise, blue and inky under the thinning skin of my legs and arms. Although I am only forty-two years old, my face is growing soft. My lips have fallen slack because I have no one to talk to anymore. I am alone in the summerhouse, and the rooms are empty and clean, vacant for years now.

I hardly remember how the lower house looked long ago because it was rented to vacationers. But the top stories were shared by my family, and so were the widow's walk and the sunroom where Wanda spoke of deep-sea divers and wild horses on Cedar Island. They wove through great glittering trails of broken glass on the shores. Sometimes a long, wavering flock flew over our house in the evenings, the shadow of the wings breaking over the roof where we stood, facing the wind.

Aunt Joan talked a lot about Wanda and wore long red dresses with powder-blue, high-heeled sandals, leather laced to her ankles, her white-painted toenails poking out the fronts. She bathed the house in rose cologne, her perfumed hair long and auburn, twisted into a high, precarious knot coiled around her head.

Whenever Aunt Joan loved a man, I knew it because she brought him to the second floor and sat him down on the black leather sofa. She would whisper something slightly obscene, then wait for him to laugh.

While he laughed, she took the pins out of her hair, then let it unravel slowly on its own. I loved the sound of her hair dropping to her hips, a swoop, a brush, and a thud. To this day, even though Joan is seventy years old and living in an asylum now, bald because the nurses shaved her, I try to fashion my hair to resemble hers that summer. I still have her old braid, auburn laced with gray, a gift from the nurses who'd shorn her. Sometimes I weave Joan's braid into my own, thinking of Wanda.

"Poor Wanda," Aunt Joan said that summer long ago, "that girl's too smart for her own good."

"What about her?" I asked, calling Aunt Joan's bluff when she first started in on Wanda.

"She learned too much at that fancy university of hers," Joan said, "and now she looks scared."

"She looks all right to me," I said, lying through my stained teeth. Wanda didn't look all right. Her hands shook, and I often heard her in the bathroom after meals, vomiting what little food she had eaten.

"Don't deny it. Why else would she quit her studies? She's ashamed as if she brushed past the ghost of Jesus in the night."

"Wanda doesn't believe in God."

"But she's still afraid of Jesus?"

"I don't know."

"She knows what she didn't want to know," Joan said, twirling her hair after dousing it with cheap perfume, "and now she's got to assimilate that knowledge and become a different person entirely or shrivel up in her room and die."

"She's the same as ever," I said, mesmerized by Joan's lovely eyes. "She'll live a long time yet."

"Uhhhhh," Joan said. "You don't know what happens to people."

Joan had violet eyes, the whites entangled with broken veins. I opened my mouth to argue with her about Wanda but stopped when I saw her eyes lit with tears.

"Hush," she whispered, "just hush up now."

So I kept quiet, wondering what Joan was really crying about in our charming summerhouse where the men waited for her on the pale balconies, smoking expensive cigarettes, the smoke that would cling to what she wore.

From her bedroom window, I watched the men, the metal lighters glaring in their fumbling hands while Joan rummaged through her twin closets. She glanced over a series of red dresses, satin, lace, and dyed muslin. Even though she was an attractive woman and no one was wearing corsets anymore, Aunt Joan had never given up the corsets her mother taught her to wear when she was a young girl. She tightened her beige corset by tying the straps to the bedposts and leaning down toward the floor, straining and sucking in air until the straps pulled tight as the silvered strings on Dougy's guitar.

Her waist was so tiny then, I wondered how she could eat. Her back was so stiff she couldn't turn all the way around to look at herself in the mirror, but she was beautiful from any angle. Her figure was the perfect hourglass I longed for.

Under her corsets, her ribs were gradually deformed, small as a child's, turning in on themselves in the years since her girlhood. Even now her nurses say she has trouble breathing. Her stomach muscles won't constrict on their own strength. Her lungs wither in their small, misshapen cage.

When I was a young girl, my body was unruly compared to Aunt Joan's. I still had baby fat around my waist and was waiting for my breasts to grow. In truth, I had no breasts and was terrified that I would never have a woman's figure. I thought I would always be pudgy around my belly and have a chest as flat as the dock rails and tiny nipples as soft as raisins. I hated my body and thought I had an ugly face. Wanda was beautiful compared to me, and I wanted to look like her. Joan was a miracle of womanhood in my eyes, and I wanted to have power over men like she did.

But I was mistaken about the power women had over men, just as I was mistaken about the power women had over their own bodies. I was wrong about many things that summer, especially when it came to Joan and Wanda. I knew nothing then.

I didn't know anything until I became a woman myself and Joan had grown old. I found out she thought her waist wasn't ever slight enough for the men's hands. Joan confessed as much to me at the asylum. She said her goal was to have a waist small enough to be completely encircled by two hands, and she almost obtained it, but not quite. Her hair was never long enough, her eyes never quite so blue.

As far back as I can remember, during my summers with Wanda, it was one man after another for Aunt Joan. Her men were the vacationers who paid to occupy the lower rooms of our house. Joan was always caught on the stairs, rushing between the first and second floors.

But her summer romances always ended in August when our family returned to the hilly neighborhoods. We were all supposed to go back to our normal lives. Wanda was expected to go back to her psychology classes. Dougy was to return to his failed jazz band and the pitiful *Walden* courses he taught at the university where Wanda studied. Father was to fall back on his investments, Mother on her charities.

I was just a girl then. School and Key Club were all I had. I didn't want the summer to end because I didn't want to lose

Wanda. She would have been the first in our family with a college education. I felt like she was outgrowing me. I feared that she hated Joan's eccentricities and resented our parents and the old folks for their simple ways.

One evening while Joan kept the men waiting, she burst into tears. "Wanda's headed for trouble," she said. "She's losing it. I think you know how I know."

It's hell for a family to know each other so well, but I don't know if we ever knew Wanda as well as we thought. Aunt Joan was the one heading for trouble every day of her life. *You don't know what happens to people,* I can still hear her say.

During the winters, Aunt Joan spoke to no one. She locked herself in her small blond-brick house on the hills and stocked up with canned peaches, waiting to be snowed in. I wasn't sure what she was doing in that house until Father, her brother, told me why he never visited her during the storms.

She had a room of mirrors I had seen many times before without knowing its function. I thought maybe she loved mirrors because she was a beautiful woman and an artist. When I was a child, I thought all great artists painted beautiful women. So I thought Aunt Joan was doubly lucky, being able to paint herself.

When I was older, Father told me she would undress in that room and draw for hours, sketching the horror she saw in the mirrors, what the corsets and diets had done to her body – bent ribs, nipples scarred from cinching, an unbalanced pelvis, pale skin marked by straps and buttons that had pressed too hard into her stomach's drooping pouch.

I know what she really looked like under her dresses

because when she had to be locked away, I was the one who unpacked her house and disposed of its contents – the easels and sketchbooks, blue paints, inkbottles and charcoal, the crumbing pastels marking my hands.

I kept the strange sketches of my aunt stripped of her disguises, completely nude, her knowing expression chastised, painfully aware of what she was. I think of how beautiful Aunt Joan was in her heels and dresses, and I can't get over the drawings, the way she saw herself all that time.

Maybe the real pity of the situation is that if she had displayed her sketches in galleries rather than her innocent renderings of whales and sunken ships, coral snakes and clown fish swimming through bluish chambers, she might have been taken seriously as an artist. Maybe she would have eventually been known as great, famous enough for her stay in the asylum to increase the market value of her work. Instead, her ocean murals are faded, peeling away like her damaged skin, painted over like her old face, her canvases disposed of in many houses. I alone know the secret of her portraits, the sketches I keep hidden under my bed.

After all this time, Aunt Joan's misshapen body is slowly replacing my memory of Wanda's natural beauty. I can't even remember Wanda's voice or her smile, although when I close my eyes I can hear Aunt Joan's weeping and see her collapsed breast, the curve of her twisted spine.

I assumed Wanda was trying to distract me from the truth.

Although at the time I had no idea what she was hiding or that one sister could so mistrust another, now I realize I betrayed her.

The whole summer was a betrayal, but at the time, I thought she was entertaining me because I was the youngest. Mostly, I just sat on the tile beneath her hammock, my back to the air vents. I watched her mouth move as Dougy smoked and Mother looked into Father's eyes. All along, our aunts and great-aunts, our grandmothers and great-grandmothers knitted blue shawls for warmth in the white winter that awaited us on the hills.

The silent veterans had scaled the seas of two wars but never spoke of violence again. They didn't speak to their wives or to one another. They sat on the porch in silence, facing the ocean. There's no telling what they were thinking, if the face of Hitler ever merged with the face of Jesus behind their eyes or if they ever knew who I was. Maybe they sensed Wanda wouldn't follow us into that winter.

My sister had a curious mouth, uneven, twisted, ripe with the color of wine berries. Her expression was serious, her gaze often still. As she looked off in the distance, her face sometimes reminded me of a large statue in a chapel garden I visited as a small child, pale stone burnished by light, etched in shadow, stained in umber mold. I thought the pupils gathered all the darkness like two black stones, until I stood closer and saw the hollow circles catching shadow. I stood on a bench so I could touch the statue's eyes and was disappointed by their simple design.

I despise my curiosity, hate needing to know how faces come together, why they change with time. But mostly I hate my desire to relive what happened to my sister, how my family was destroyed as our tiny failures collected into huge sorrow. I don't delight in old wounds although I trace the scars at night, leaving the house's doors open for anyone to come inside. I never lock up. I never turn anyone away, not even the drifters who follow the coast to nowhere.

I confess everything, the way my family disappointed each other, until no one would look me in the eye without a glint of pain, sudden accusations wordless on the hot air. At first, no one knew where the sorrow was coming from, why it descended upon us like the shadow of a great wave darkening across blue water. One thing I've never figured out is how to make the sorrow go away without sending a part of myself along with it.

By the time the deepest depression left with Wanda, following her away from the summerhouse, far from our sheltered lives, she left me numb in the wake of her absence. I was never whole without her. When she left, she took the best of me with her, probably never realizing what she had done.

I felt like I was touching a woman made of stone the evening I held Wanda's wrist near the high open windows of the summerhouse. On the vacant third floor where the guests used to sleep, Wanda wore a thin green nightgown, long and sleeveless with bright yellow patches near her knees. At the windows, she stood in the strangest pose, her palms touching; her fingers laced together, her arms held high, so that her right arm hid her eyes. Her face rested under the crook of her arm, as if she were rubbing sleep from her eyes or shading them from moonlight. She might have been ashamed or cringing against the salty air.

As much as she liked to talk during the days, she was often silent by evening. She didn't respond to my hand on her wrist, so I drew away from her. She might have been a cruel stranger disguised as Wanda, an impostor who destroyed my sister then took her place in the summerhouse. But she was probably just Wanda, my sister slowly growing strange, her sandy skin aglow under the soft light of fluted lamps.

Outside the window, giant dunes rose from blue darkness, the ocean one with the night sky. Lighthouse beacons pierced the distance. That night, like every night, the breeze smelled of dead fish writhing on the sand, their eyes drying on dank air, fins and oily flesh that would smolder in morning sun, shells that rolled out too far, trapping snails on the shore.

There was nothing to see but all that darkness, tiny moths beating themselves to death on the screen, the dull powder their wings left behind. Crickets leaped and flailed below us.

"What it is?" I asked, tugging at Wanda's gown.

"Look," she said, "on the sand."

"I don't see anything."

"There." She pressed her face against the screen.

"Where?"

I squinted until my eyes played tricks on me. I saw aqua lights on glinting waves and sand crabs scattering like roaches scaling moonlit grains. A houseboat drifted sideways. A pack of stray dogs leaped off the dock, rooting through trash barrels, the vacationers' refuse. Cluttered papers whirled into the water.

"Those dogs?" I asked, clawing at the screen.

She turned around to me, her eyes looking sad, unfocused. "You all think I'm crazy," she said. "You think I'm making this up."

Covering her left eye with her hand, she gazed out the window in the direction of the dock pillars, the coarse ropes that tied wooden bridges to the shore.

I don't know why she was always looking outside when the house was so wonderful inside, the rooms brightly painted by Aunt Joan, lit with shell lamps dyed pink and teal, their bearded fringe beaded, clacking all through the night. Record players turned in every bedroom, weaving old jazz into show tunes, opera and banjo lacing together through the halls. All along the walls, purple and gray murals of marlins rose out of painted water, the *Queen Anne's Revenge* rendered in great detail, a hall of blue waves etched along the ceiling, a floor of green tiles sparkling under our feet.

"This is our house," I used to say to myself as I walked to my room at night. "This is our house, and I live here with Wanda."

Then I didn't say it anymore.

"I hate it here," Wanda said one night, leaning her forehead against the window screen, her expression hidden from me. Our last summer together, she got in the habit of standing like that all night, waiting until first light before descending the curved stairs to her room, stumbling all the way to her bed where Dougy caught her.

*　　　*　　　*

Dougy carried the sickness to the heart of my sorrow. I feared I was losing Wanda to him, and he was the last person I ever wanted to lose her to. She was too good for him, and I thought he knew it. He was letting himself rot, and I could smell him in the halls outside of Wanda's room.

Almost forty years old by the time he found his place in American literature, Dougy wore a farmer's denim overalls without a shirt underneath and never bathed. He had a long beard, dark and tangled, matted with spilled wine and specks of putrefied hamburger meat. He was slowly drinking himself to death, but I didn't know what he was doing that summer. I had never watched anyone die that way before.

Sometimes his eyes wouldn't focus and his words wouldn't make sense. Once I watched him pick a minuscule worm from his chin as if it were nothing, crushing it in the coarse hairs where it writhed. What Wanda ever saw in him I never knew, except for the fact that he used to be her professor and she was three months pregnant with his child. But no one ever spoke of that, at least not to me. Through my bedroom walls late at night, I often heard Mother arguing with Wanda and Dougy about the baby when everyone else was sleeping.

"Guess I'm just a lover and a fool," Dougy used to say to Mother, "pretty much a dead ringer for Walt Whitman. At least that's what people tell me."

He worshipped the Transcendentalists and taught classes on Emerson and Thoreau, often weeping as he read passages from

Walden to my sister.

I once heard Father say to Mother, "Dougy is a bastard, and I don't mean he never knew his real father. I mean he has the soul of a bastard and wants to destroy the world."

As much as Dougy loved nature and freedom, he never wrote about anything that didn't lead to hookers imprisoned in dark rooms. His tattered manuscript was a series of sestinas about Venetian whorehouses, French sisters, and drunken Texans.

He especially liked to make fun of the old folks because, while the veterans smoked cigarettes and drank coffee on the deck, their wives spent their days fighting over tiny details of the past. Dougy could easily confuse them. The women never understood who he really was. They didn't know why he lived with us in the summerhouse. They had no idea where Dougy came from or why men waited for Aunt Joan on the balconies.

The old folks couldn't have accepted that Wanda slept with a man in her room because they remembered her, but only as a child. Sometimes they thought I was Wanda, and that wasn't really so bad. The worst days were when they forgot their own names.

Maybe Dougy loved talking to aged women because they didn't understand his failure. They had lost control of most of their bodily functions long ago, so how could he have been ashamed of anything with them?

"I love old broads," he used to say. "They really dig me."

But I didn't think it was funny. All the old folks are dead now. The summerhouse was rightfully their house, but they never understood what was happening inside. They never knew who Dougy was, and they never knew who I was. I only caught them at the end of their lives and saw their worst days when they had no dignity and I had no way of knowing what type of people they once were.

"Who is this girl?" one of the great-aunts asked every day that summer. But I could never explain to any of them who I really was.

Sometimes I was afraid, imagining Wanda's face hidden forever, her nose and mouth lost in the shadow of her arm. Before nightfall, I often stood outside the house for hours, never swimming or walking along the sand. I waited at the gate, gazing up at Wanda, wondering what she saw. But what does it matter now? I was only twelve years old, too young to realize Wanda's behavior fascinated me for all the wrong reasons.

I thought I could see what she saw. I thought if I looked long enough I could discover what was waiting outside the window. Sometimes I still think there's something out there, something that only Wanda saw but no one else could see. Now, whenever I drink my gin in darkness, I hold my glass high and think, *Here's hoping she had wonderful eyes.* At least, my fondest wish is that she gave me up for something real, not what she imagined.

Now that the others are gone, I live here in the summerhouse alone. The beaches have changed and grown more crowded every year. But I'm still afraid to look out the windows at night – not because someone might be lurking outside but because I see nothing but the dark shore and yet feel so much terror I have to stand at the windows until dawn. I don't want to be like Wanda, a woman afraid of sleeping in the dark.

Dougy was a slave to her fears, and so was I. But I was nothing like him. He drank three bottles of cheap wine every night and tried to force Wanda to do the same so she would take her clothes off and dance on the shore. I hated Dougy and wanted him to die a lingering death underwater. In the afternoons, he made my sister laugh like a whore, her mouth gaping wet, laced with spit strings, full of glittery darkness. Her laughter was followed by long silences.

"Here," Dougy would often say, "take this."

Once he offered me a bottle of stale wine, a gob of kinky hairs floating on the burgundy liquor. The label was peeling away, leaving gold traces on his palms. Flecks of metallic paper caught in his tangled beard and nestled deep into the corners of his lips.

Wanda ignored him and walked to the window. The sun was still high. A group of children ran out into the water, screaming and shoving one another farther from the shore.

"Want to go outside?" he asked, his nose buried in her hair. She didn't answer. I watched his eyes glaze over, gazing at me cruelly before he guzzled the last wine, stray hairs and all. He relaxed his fingers, letting the bottle drop to the carpet before kicking it across the room.

"What?" he asked, looking at me strangely.

"I didn't say anything."

"All right, then."

*   *   *

Later that night, Wanda and I were silent as we watched the moonlit shore from the high windows. Dougy took possession of our aunt in darkness without ever bothering to remove her corset. The ocean was lapping their legs. Joan shouted obscenities as Dougy mounted her like a crazed horse and she arched her back, stiff as a mechanical doll. When she finally shouted my father's name, Dougy jerked away from her.

Afterward, Dougy ran back to the house, yanking at his jeans. Joan lay on the shore for a long time, her face in the sand.

Somehow Wanda was never the same after that night. Neither was I or the summerhouse or the rest of the family. I have no idea who else might have seen Joan and Dougy through the other windows or what my parents and the old folks might have heard.

I didn't know what to say to Wanda when she finally left the window and turned to me. I tried to hug her, but she pushed me away.

"The people I love don't exist anymore and haven't for quite some time," she said, "even though they still live with me in the same house."

When I reach for the family album, the photos are almost too much for me. I'll burn them before I die, before I have to think of my sister curled up in the long hammock, the white woven cords stretched tight under her weight. Her skin was luminous, shades lighter than her hair. When I look back at summer photographs, Wanda standing just behind me, my head barely reaching the crook of her arm, I see now what I couldn't have realized then. My sister and I looked nothing alike. She was on the verge of becoming a great beauty. Her thick auburn hair curved, glistening dark above her white gown, her breasts huge in mellow light. My hair was dishwater-blond, limp, and dull. My skin, the color of petrified bone. My breasts, nonexistent. I was just a girl then. But in the photographs, I could have been an ashen, long-haired boy, a child living a sheltered life to serve her, walking with her violet pitcher of iced cranberry juice from room to room in sickly light.

I would like to say it was a long time ago, but, as Wanda used to say, even a hundred years isn't a long time. She had a comic timeline on her wall in the summerhouse, a line of figures representing human evolution as a series of shaggy apes growing hairless through the ages. Unlike my sister, I've never known the first thing about time. I wasn't like the old folks either. I had no history to call my own. I was only ever aquatinted with the tiniest details, the useless moments no one else would bother to remember.

I still only hold on to the smallest memories because of their gemlike quality. When I strand them together, they could reveal Wanda's most intimate secrets or nothing at all. Nevertheless, they are beautiful to me, just as valuable as the lessons Wanda learned in her psychology classes. She learned how to take people apart, studying their lives as confessions to unconscious desires until even her closest friends became strangers to her.

She told me there was only ever one history, hers and mine, and it happened again and again. According to Wanda, life was whatever we chose to make of it, like the two broken mauve goblets she lifted from a junkyard and displayed prominently in her bright room. Romance was the same since the dawn of time – a man offers a woman all he will ever possess so she will become his slave.

As Wanda reclined in the hammock against brown velvet pillows, her gold necklace suspending a rectangle of green glass, I reached out for a cracked goblet and saw its veins stained in burgundy wine.

"Don't," she said, not looking at me. She was reading a thick white book on how to make love, and "don't" was the only word she had spoken to me all morning.

"Dougy's ugly and I hate him and Aunt Joan," I said.

"You're so sweet," she whispered.

The book was cumbersome and full of black-and-white photos of naked people, women with heavy, drooping breasts and slender waists and men with fat stomachs and hairy legs. But I wasn't looking at the men. I was looking at the women. I wanted to hold them and bury my face in their hair. That was the moment I realized I could never love a man. I could only love women all of my life, and I would always remember I was studying Wanda as she studied her book on love.

I learned nothing about romance that summer, nor did I ever learn. The closest I ever came was my admiration for Wanda and the chipped mauve goblets, the marred crystal rims that cut my hand once.

I used to watch Wanda pluck her eyebrows with tweezers, shaping them into sideways silver moons. I rubbed lotion on her legs and arms, lingering over her breasts and knees, so the heat wouldn't dry her skin. I helped her rinse her hair in vinegar, eggs, and beer. After smearing a blue-cream mask over her face, she clambered back onto the hammock and asked me to lay cucumber slices over her eyes.

"I want to look as irresistible as Aunt Joan," she said to me before beginning a grueling regime of home-beauty treatments.

Our last night together, I watched her wallow in a tub full of olive oil. I poured it in a slow stream over her shoulders so her skin could drink of its richness. Her hair stuck to her skin in a flat and glossy web. She was falling all over herself as she tried to rise from that tub, her feet sliding out from under her so she had to hold on to me. I grabbed her arms as she stood, but her wrists were so slick with oil that they began to slip through my hands. Or rather, I let them slip.

"Oh, God," she said, laughing as she clung to me. My shirt was ruined, soaked in oil.

Dougy was waiting outside the door, laughing and demanding to take a picture of Wanda while she was still wet and luminous. She was so beautiful that night he forgot to put film in his camera. She was laughing and holding on to my shoulders when he snapped the shot.

"I love you. God, I love you," she said, her arms wrapped around my waist as she kissed my hair. I didn't believe her, so I pushed her away instead of returning her embrace. That would be the last time we held each other.

Later that night, naked and alone, she went for a walk along the beach and jumped off a bridge near our house. No one saw her go. Her face had always been so lovely that it didn't make sense the way strangers found her, her head next to a shattered melon on the rocks, dark blood mingling with the bridge's shadow.

I wasn't allowed to see her face at the closed-coffin funeral where Dougy tried to open the casket, begging to touch her hair one last time. Father wouldn't let him touch her – neither would Mother and neither would I.

Aunt Joan was leaning against me, her hands on my shoulders. I knew the old folks were standing behind us, but I couldn't bear to look back at them. As far as I could tell, none of us could stand to look at one another. No one would speak to me during the wake, so I began to speak to myself in a voice so soft no one else could hear me.

I told myself I would have followed my sister to the edge of any shore. But I couldn't have believed she would have taken her own life. I was searching for some other explanation for why she never came back home. I never found one.

She seemed truly happy that night. She had a baby inside her that no one would ever see. Lovely as she was, she was laughing, and so was I, even though I felt her arms slipping through my hands.

THE ANSWER

Will someone make the birds go away? Will the winds die down? Will the house on the dunes be swept ashore? What is romance? What is a heartbeat? What is this poison in the blue bottle that smells like flames?

Where is the knife? Where is the hammer? What is burning? When do Daddy's dark eyes ever close? When does he turn aside? How do I stop this? When will it end? Will anyone try to find us? Where has Daddy gone? Why did he have to go away?

Why did the house catch fire? Who let the carpets go black?

Did the gun go off?

Do your hands smell like ashes? Why are there ashes on my hands?

Where am I?

Why is the ceiling blue like the sky?

Will someone make the leaves fall? Will someone mend the crack in the glass? Will someone put the milk away before it sours? Why does it sour? Where is the cow that the milk came

from? Who milked it? Where did we get the money to buy it?
How much did it cost? Where did it come from?

See this bruise around my sister's eye? How did it
get there? What is a bruise? Why is it purple and blue
surrounded by a red ring? Why can't she open that eye?
Will the skin turn yellow or green? Will it fall away? When
will it stop hurting when I touch it? What's wrong with my
eyes?

Is it wrong to touch my eye? Can I touch her eyes?

Will someone make the man stop laughing? Will
someone wake Daddy? Will someone sing a song? What's his
favorite song? Don't you remember?

Does anybody hear me? Why isn't anyone looking at
me?

Will the woman in the black dress ever turn her eyes
away from the fire? Will the fire ever stop burning?

What is there to drink? Where has the milk gone?
What's wrong with it? Can I have a glass of water? Where is the
ice? What am I to eat? Where do I sleep? Isn't there room
enough in the house for me?

Will anyone answer me? Why not?

What's wrong?

What time is it? Is the clock fast? Will it just keep
ticking? How long? Has it been an hour? How many hours?
How long will I be here? When can I go home? Will I ever go
home? Where's home?

Has the house gone away?

Is Mommy still in the garage? What is she doing there? Can I go to her? Why can't I hear her anymore? What was she trying to say? What did she mean to tell me? What does *brazen* mean? What is *depraved mind*?

Can the woman in the black dress dance? Can she make toast? Can she sew a pretty pillow and clap loudly with her smooth hands? Why is she wearing Mommy's rings? Where did she get them? Did Daddy give them to her?

Who will drink the moonshine? Who will watch the still? Who will feed the chickens in the morning? Can I? Can I throw the corn high into the dust and watch them peck away?

Will she watch me? What is she doing with her long dress? Why does she have to take it off? What's the matter with her? Why is she crying? Who is she? Where did she come from? Why is she here? Why am I?

When will Daddy tell us to go home? When will Daddy walk again?

What's in the garage? Why can't I go there?

Why is the man with the beard shaving it off? Why does his face look different now? Can I have his beard when he's done with it? Will he let me keep it? Or does he want the hairs? Where will he keep them? What will he do with them?

Can I hold the gun for a little while? Can I touch it? Can I play with it for just a minute and give it back to him?

Why is the woman's dress on the floor? Why are her arms shaking? Why is she so afraid of the gun? Won't she look at me? Does she know my name? Can I tell it to her? Does she like me?

What's Cissy doing here?

Where did she get that gauze? Why was her wedding canceled? Will the church bells ever quit ringing? Do they ring for her?

Where is the man who was to be her husband? Where are the bride's maids? Why are the straps falling off her shoulders? Why are her breasts so red and small, her nipples entangled in the black beads?

Can I patch her dress with some white muslin? Does she want me to mend it and make it right for another wedding, another church, another groom? What happened to the first one? Where is he now? Why did he leave her? Why has he gone away?

Won't someone ever marry her? Why not?

Can she marry a woman someday? Does it have to be a man?

Why?

Will I still get to catch the flowers? Will she throw them to me? Will I get to wear pink taffeta? Will the organ play? Will she walk down the aisle? Will the boys' choir ring the bells?

Will my sister sing again?

Why is Cissy tossing her shoes in the sink full of blood? What has she done with the knife? Why was Daddy after her? Why was he lost in the hotel? Why was she hiding upstairs in the dark? What was she waiting for?

How did she know about the fire? Why did she come down for us?

Why is the woman reaching for the black dress, her bare hips so soft and so white against the blue floor? Why is she rubbing her face against the gold rug?

Why is my sister staring at the wall? Why doesn't she answer me? Why is her yellow shirt torn?

Why are people full of blood? How much blood is in a person? Why is it red? Why is it dark and crusty like rust when it dries? What happens when it runs out? Will it ever wash away?

Why is Cissy touching my hair? Does she have to braid it so tight? Will she leave me alone if I ask her? Should I ask her?

Why is the woman afraid of her? Why did Cissy cut my sister's arms? Why did the little man give me his beard?

Do you think it smells like smoke?

Now that he has put the hairs in my hands, what do I do with them? Even after I roll them into a little ball, why do they all start to unwind and fall away? Why are they kinky, prickly like the grasses?

Will the grasses ever stop growing? How high will they get? Who let them grow up higher than the windows? How does the moonlight make its way through the grasses? Will we die in this house?

What is Cissy doing here? Was this supposed to be her house? Does she want to live here? Does she want to keep us here with her?

Why did she take the beard away? Can't I have it anymore? Does my sister want it? When Cissy puts the beard into my sister's lap, why does my sister start to cry – howling, not moaning softly like the woman who reaches out to her bandaged arms?

Who put the bandages on her? Will she ever stop bleeding?

Can I sew her arms with my needle and thread? Will she let me? Will it make her better if she does? Will she love me more? Will I be her favorite then?

Jeanette? Jeanette, can you hear me?

Do you hear the bubbles moving in Daddy's stomach? Why does the little man think it's funny? Why is he smiling at me as if I understand a joke he's told just for me? Why is he reaching out for me?

Must I go to him? What if I don't want to? Will he punish me? Will Daddy let him? Is he stronger than Daddy?

Does Daddy still see us? What's wrong with his eyes? Why doesn't he blink anymore? Will he stare forever, always looking in the same direction? Will someone close his eyes for him? Can I? If I close them, will they ever open? Will he look at me forever if I stand in front of him? What if I don't want him to always see me this way?

What if I move? Will his eyes follow me across the room? Why? When I strike the long match, why does it flare? Can I blow it out? Can I wave it in front of my sister's eyes? Does Cissy like the fire?

Does the little man love me like he loves Cissy? Will he kiss my hand forever? If I ask him, will he let go? What if I don't want to live anymore? Will he ever quit touching me? If I'm dead, will he leave me alone?

Will someone give me a violet velvet kite and let me fly it across the morning sky? When does the sun come up?

What is the dawn? Why is it so beautiful, the way it lights the sky? Why do the clouds change colors? Why does the moon go away? Where does it go? Is it hiding? Does it always come back? Why? Where do all the stars go? Are they sad when they have to go away?

Will someone feed me? What color are my eyes?

Do you like my hair? Do I have pretty hair? Prettier than my sister's? Prettier than Cissy's? Does it look like Mommy's?

Who are they talking to? Why don't you listen? Where are you? Where have you gone? Why do you have to go away?

Cissy, can I have a sandwich? Cissy, why do you smoke those cigarettes that make you cough? Can I light them for you? Can I play with the lighter? Why does the little flame split in two? What makes it dance in your blue eyes? Cissy, can I marry you? Will you let me be your new husband?

Did the yellow pills taste like chalk? Did they make you sleepy? Did I give you bad dreams?

Do you want to burn me? Is it because I ask too many questions? Why do you think I do it?

Are you angry? Why? What have I done?

Did the silver car break down? Why did we leave it on the highway? Will someone find it and fix it and bring it back to us? Will we go back for it someday?

If I'm good, will you make me another dolly? If I'm quiet, will you give her a white dress and long hair? Will she be a bride doll? Will you sew the groom? Can they kiss in the night?

What are you doing to my sister?

Where did the little man go? Where is all that music coming from? When the house caught fire, were you there? Where did my sister go when I had to wake her in the night? Why wasn't she dreaming? Why did she try to run away? Did she try to take me with her? Can she and I go away now?

Can I have a biscuit? Can I have blueberries with sugar? Where did the wine go? Where is the red? Where is the white? Who drank all of Daddy's wine? What did it taste like, the grapes that rotted on the vines long after the rains? Can I have the candles?

Who will put the wicks out when all of the wax melts away? Can we make new pink candles with flower petals and snowflake patterns etched in the wax and magazine photos trapped inside so that the pictures become clear as they burn away?

Do you want to talk about the fire?

Am I a good girl? Am I nice? Am I an angel?

Will the little man teach me how to make soap? Will he sculpt tiny statues of women out of lard and sell them at the county fair? Will he paint with ashes, making pictures of the gray-blue sea?

Will we ever go there, Jeanette? Can I go with you? Will I ever be married? Would I make a good wife? Will any man want me after what's happened? Can I change my name and make up a new history? Can we start a new life and leave this one behind? Would you like that as much as you like me?

Am I smart? Am I amazing? Will I be a scientist someday? Will I be a doctor or a doctor's wife? Am I a capable girl? Who will dress me in the mornings? What shall I wear? Am I old enough to dress myself? When will I be?

Why is the gate open? Why have the workmen torn up the trail past Stray Horn? Can we go back to the pond? Do we have to go the long way? Cissy, is it too late? Can I swim today? Is there some way I can get a little piece of gum? Who will run the bath water? Can I have bubbles that smell like irises? Will the perfume smell of tulips, mimosa blossoms, honeysuckle, or yellow roses?

Who will water the rose garden? When will the rains come? Can I walk with you across the highway? Which way do all the cars go? What are they escaping?

Will it be a long night? Do you need any help with Mommy? Can I watch her for you? Are you afraid of fire? Why can't we play with fire? What does that mean? What is fire? What makes it burn? How do you play with it? Have you ever before?

Did Mommy break her legs? Where did she go? Do you want me to try to find her? Can Jeanette go after her like she went after the lost kittens in the evening?

Can I be beautiful like you? Can you be small like me? Can't we be friends? Will someone feed the scarlet macaw? Will someone shoot the black bear? Will someone write my name in the sand? Will my sister flex her toes before dancing the tango? Will Daddy play guitar? Will Mommy knit a sweater?

When will we travel across the ocean? When will we escape across the sea? Is the river too rough for us? Is the stream too narrow? Will we live on the lakeshore? Is that the place for Daddy to find us?

Did Cissy shoot the dogs? Did the rabbit die? Why did it have red eyes? Why are my sister's eyes gray?

After I brush my teeth, why does the cat put its nose in my mouth and sniff inside? Why does my sister always keep her hair dry in the bath? Will someone brush my teeth? Will someone make blue-glass candy? Can I crack it with the knife handle? Who will brush the cat's teeth? Is she an angel?

Can I look at Cissy's teeth? Can I have a cigarette? Can I flick her lighter? Shall I examine Daddy's face under the light? Can we go to the movies? Who will buy the tickets? Before tea, who will make the water boil?

Jeanette, will you tell me stories? Will Daddy saw down the dead tree? Will Mommy bake potatoes and ham? Will my sister brush her hair? Will I grow old? Will I grow hungry? Where will I rest my head? On the stone? Will the woman with the black dress get her dress back? Will the little man hush her crying? Will Cissy find the knife and start another fire? Will I become a woman if I live through another night? Has the little man made me a woman yet?

Shall I change my dress? Shall I change my hair?

Where are the keys to the house? What is behind that door? Why is it locked? Has the groom locked himself inside? Did he bend the bars on the window wanting to get away?

Can I play checkers? Can I cheat?

Does that ring mean anything? Why is it on her finger?

Has the water boiled? Has the chestnut tea grown cold? Who will tend the strawberry patch? Who will plow the fields? Who will teach me how to read a book, how to catch a fish, how to paint a face like the moon? If I go, will Cissy follow me? Will you, little man?

Who is that whimpering? Where does the whimpering come from? Little man, can you hear it, too? Does it frighten you like me? Little man, why are you so little? Can you really be a man? Why are you with us? What is that scar on your face, lip to chin? How did you get it? Why are your teeth silver?

Who is that girl tattooed across your arm? Can I touch her? When you flex your muscles, does her hair grow longer? Will you make your muscle bounce? How does she change like that, from woman to child, from child to woman, and back again just like me?

Where is the phone? Can I make a call? Shall I call my friend Susan? Do you want her to play with us?

Where is the radio? Shall I close my eyes and try to find you? Where are the keys to the car? Can I see them? If we scream real loud, can anyone hear us? Does anyone know we're here? Whose house is this anyway? Where is the prison? How far is it from here? Do you know the sheriff? Is he looking for us now? When will he start looking? Does anyone know we're gone?

Little man, where did you get your hat? Why are your fingernails long like Cissy's? Is there a dog in the woodshed? Is there an ax? Why did you paint it green? If I paint your nails with the pink-shell polish, will you paint mine candy-apple red?

How did you strain your arm? Will someone make the pain go away? Shall I kiss it and make it better? How's that?

Am I a good girl? Did I do a good thing?

Who's that in the photographs on the wall? Is that the woman in the black dress? Can I put the dress back on her? Why are her ankles so small? Why is there water around her mouth? Why are there scratches around her eyes? Why are her legs so soft and so warm like cotton pillows?

Did you see what happened to Mommy's scarves? Did you see the wave ornaments in the windows? Did they burn in the fire?

Little man, can I kiss your mouth? Can I kiss your feet, your toes one at a time? Can I comb the blood out of your hair? Will Cissy let me? Am I allowed to hug your neck? If I do what you say, will Daddy talk again? If I'm nice to you, will you let me go away?

Are you the handsomest man in the world? Will I ever find a husband as good as you? Will I ever be as beautiful as Cissy, as clever as her? Do you believe I will do anything you want me to do? Did you know I know how to kiss, how to sing, how to dance, how to strip, how to hike my panties up to make them look like a string bikini?

But how do I tremble like the woman in the black dress? Did you know I can be like her? Will you teach me how?

Did you know I'd do whatever you say? Can I be your best friend? Can I be Cissy's little girl? Is that what you want me to be? Do you want me to be your wife? Would you like it if I married you? Can I see Mommy then? Will Daddy get up and walk away?

Do you like my dress? Do you want me to take it off? Do you want me to dance for you like a little ballerina in a jewelry box? Do you think I'm pretty? If I'm nice to you, will you leave my sister alone? Will you let her go away?

Can I go with her? Is my sister all right? What's happened to her? Why can't she hear me? Why does she keep turning away? Don't you know she loves you? Don't you believe me? Don't you know she loves you more than anyone else in the world? Will someone make a statue of you someday? Will someone paint your picture? Would you like it if I painted it?

Are you an artist, too? Did you paint that white star in the rain? Is it for sale? Can I buy it? How much does it cost? Where are your paints and brushes? Can I see them? Can I paint a rainbow on the walls? Do you like rainbows? Have you ever seen a real one before?

Sister, do you remember that storm? Sister, can you hear me? Can you stand up? Will you be nice to the little man now? If we're nice to him, will he be nice to us? Isn't that the way?

Don't you think he's handsome? Will you give him a kiss like I did? See how easy it is? See how nice he can be? Will you sit on his lap now? Can I hug you? Sister, aren't you glad we're still alive?

Did you forget to thank the little man?

Will you tell him you love him? Will you tell him you're sorry? Sister? Do you feel my hand on your hand? Can you feel it on your face? Why are you breathing so hard? Why is there sweat under your arms? Are you cold? Why are you shivering? Do you want a blanket so I can make you warmer? Can I go find one?

Am I allowed to go into the other rooms? Can I look in the garage? Is Mommy still there? Why not?

Sister, do you remember me? Do you know who I am? What is my name? How old am I? What's my favorite color? Can you still hum? Can you whistle? Will you nod your head if you hear me? Will you squeeze my hand? Did the little man hurt you? Why do you flinch when he touches you? Why do you sniffle and cry? What's so terrible? Aren't you glad I'm with you?

Are you sad for the woman on the floor? Did you like it how I helped her with her dress? Will you ever stop looking at her? What's wrong? Do you know who she is? Do you know her name? Do you think she'll be all right? We'll all be all right, won't we?

Why does the roof leak? Where do the crows go? Why do the robins go away in the winter? When will they come back? Aren't they the first signs of spring? When will spring be? Can you wait for the robins? Won't that be nice? Won't we be happy then? What happens to the nests when the blue eggs hatch and the birds fly away?

Do you remember that one summer when we tried to save the baby robins in the pear tree? Why could we only save one? Why did one of them live while the other one died? Why, in the same nest, did the mother only feed one and let the other one starve, chirping during the feeding times? Is nature cruel? Was it our fault? Did we do something wrong?

Isn't the house like a nest? Isn't every house? Are we safe inside?

Will the wind tear the barn down? Will a tornado come? How much damage can the wind do? Is it stronger than we are? Can it blow right through us?

Sister, don't you know I love you? Do you love me, too? Can I brush your hair? Can I put your arms around the little man's neck? Do you like him better now? Do you believe he won't hurt us?

Can you look at his eyes? Don't you think they're beautiful? Do you like his teeth? Do you like his tattoo? Do you think he has a good laugh? Do you like the way he smiles?

Will you love him forever? Do you want to marry him, too? Do you want to have his babies like I do? Can we love him enough? If we are nice to him, won't we always be happy?

Where did Cissy go? What is she doing in the other rooms? Is everything all right with her? Can I help her clean the house? Can I go to her?

Is it time for Mommy to come out of the garage and sit with us?

Why is the woman in the black dress wearing Mommy's earrings? Why are Mommy's combs in her hair? Do you think her face looks like Mommy's? If she is Mommy, why is her hair a different color?

Sister, what are you thinking about? Do you know we're here?

Do you remember a house just like this one? Didn't it look just the same? Why did we leave? Where did we go? Doesn't Jeanette know? Remember what she told us? How could Jeanette steer us wrong?

How could you forget? Do you think the little man wants to know? Should I tell him what happened to Jeanette's hands when she broke the window?

Do you think the shards hurt her even now? Is the glass still trapped under her veins? Does the pain ever go away? Do the shards grind against her bones?

Can you see her now the way she was, the lily scarf wrapped modestly around her hair?

Cissy, if you are such a good girl, how could it be your fault? Why did you come back to us?

Did you know Jeanette said they looked everywhere in your house, turning over the wardrobe? Don't you see they only wanted to see what you saw?

Don't you know at first they only wanted to help you?

What's happened to you?

Don't you know people were trying to save you?

Cissy, if my sister is so much bigger than the little man, why is he stronger than her? Why is he holding her down so long? Will he ever let her go? Can I have her back now? Will he ever set her back on the floor with the woman in the black dress?

Woman, Woman, why is your dress so black? Is it silk? Why is it so soft? Can I touch it? Did you sew it yourself? Where did you buy it?

What's that black paint dripping like oil from your eyes? Why is your hair so tangled? How did you burn your wrists?

Do you like apples dipped in honey? Do you like cloves? Do you like wine?

Why are you wearing Mommy's earrings? Who gave them to you?

Mommy? What happened to you in the garage? What made you look so different?

Where did you get that black dress? Did Cissy give it to you? Did she tell you to put it on? Did the little man tell you to take it off?

If there was a fire, would you put it out? If there was a door, would you open it? If there was a car, would you drive away? If Daddy spoke to you softly, would you start to cry again? Would you talk to me? Would you sing to me?

Am I still your little girl? Are you or aren't you my mommy? Mommy, is it you?

What's wrong with your face? Did someone hurt it?

Will you stand?

Aren't you stronger than the little man? Aren't you bigger than him? Together with Sister and me, won't the three of us outnumber him? Won't we be stronger? Do you really think he'd be able to stop us if we tried?

Mommy, are you listening? Do you hear me?

Why can't we try?

II

SMILE, THAT'S WHY HE LOVES HER

There's one thing you'll say I've done wrong. So, I'll start with the names I've called him: Cupie Wingbow, Kissy Boy, Bustaman, Angel Bo Dienger, Waniel, Woener, Wiener Boy Piener, Dupus. (Yes, Dupus.) Are those all the names? No, but you have the idea. And what was I thinking the first time I said them? I don't know. They were just sounds that came from my mouth fifteen years ago when I held him. He was too young to know they weren't normal and would stay with him for a lifetime.

I'm the one who made sure they weren't forgotten, and that kind of remembering isn't easy in this world where for years and years people recycle the same names to give to their children. Does Angel Boy like the names? No, but you weren't the one. You weren't the oldest child in a house full of dolls and children. You didn't see him there, folded in my sister's arms. Launa also loved him for what he was, the youngest and the last and the only boy.

Don't try to tell me what I've done wrong, why he loves her more. Over the phone, you've told me therapy can change everything, erase depression, make terror go away. But what if I don't want to change even one memory that has made me who I

135

am? You and I have been friends eleven years, ever since grade school, but not long enough for you to understand me, to accept me for who I am. You didn't dream my dreams. You barely even know my sister, my brother. You didn't watch them grow. You didn't roll new words off your tongue to give Angel Boy names that have never been shared by others. Neither did Launa.

You didn't give him bad dreams. I did. When he was three years old, Dupus's first nightmare was about a naked lady he saw out his window. At night, he had to get up from his bed to go to the bathroom. He looked out the window, and he thought he saw her – starving arms, long hair waving around a face that was glowing. She was me, but I wasn't looking in his window. Even now, I like to go into his room at night when he's sleeping and listen to him breathing, my hair falling over his face. Sometimes he flinches if he wakes up and sees me standing over him. Only, I usually don't disturb him. Angel Boy usually doesn't know I'm standing there.

When Bo Dienger was four years old, I wasn't a part of his nightmares anymore. On nights of full moons, he would come to me and say that the wind on the curtains was a blue harlequin whispering through his window. I gave him red, plastic necklaces that sparkled to ward off the blue light. Only now Kissy Boy doesn't believe me when I tell him how he used to beg to wear my gowns then. He just doesn't remember, or claims he doesn't.

Mom and Dad wouldn't let Bustaman wear the gowns, so I had to find the next best thing. I took the bolt of red satin out of my closet, the one I was going to use to sew doll clothes, and made him a long cape. By the time the cape fell apart on his shoulders, Dupus had forgotten all about the naked lady, the blue harlequin, and wanting his sister's gowns.

Cupie Wingbow almost broke my hand once. You know he's older now, fifteen years old. Maybe you've heard his voice in the background and seen him walking, his hulking form sheltered under the roof. What I've been telling him all these years has made him strong. The muscles on his hairless chest and arms have nothing to do with his bench press, the punching bag in the garage, or the weights he lifts. I willed him to be strong. I told him he would be, and now he is.

My Angel Boy doesn't have to come to me. Even now, when I call him, he just won't come, but I go to him just the same. It takes that kind of love to make a boy strong. He needs one sister who loves him too much, one who doesn't love him enough. Believe me, Cupic will come away from a childhood spent with me and Launa with a certain appreciation for women that most men will never have.

Waniel is almost six feet tall now, and he has a shadow mustache, so people just don't believe him when he says he's fifteen years old. And Launa, it's the same with her when she tells people they didn't see her in a magazine. Launa, you really have to feel sorry for her. I've known her so long sometimes I forget she has a lovely, blank face and a long, lank body like a mannequin draped in fashionable clothing. Looking like a plastic girl in an old shop window, she calls our brother Dale, and he goes into her room at night to watch her curl her hair. Woener breathes deeply when she sprays the perfume on her shoulders. They laugh a lot in there. Only you wouldn't think that most of what they say is very funny.

Poor Launa, not many people will ever see her the way she really was. Remember how she looked when we were younger? Her teeth were kind of bucked out, and she was fat and had really, really kind of white hair. Yes, come to think of it, her hair was whiter than her teeth. People just don't realize how her skin wouldn't tan then. She's so fair that her skin would just go red. Her hair would just go white. When she sat down, there were three folds of skin on her belly.

Wingbow doesn't come into my room anymore and watch me like he does Launa, but I'm busy tonight, and I couldn't really talk to him like I should if he came in here anyway.

Do you remember the painting I've been working on – the castle on the cliff?

There's also the white moon, but most of the painting is a mint-green sea dapple-shadowed blue. The acrylics I'm using are the cheap kind, and the camel's hair of the brush keeps coming off on the canvas – short, straight hairs preserved as the paint dries. But you can't see the hairs unless you get close, and you know you're really supposed to look at paintings from far away.

I also keep sketchbooks and large drawings done in ink or charcoal or Prismacolors. Whenever a drawing turns out, my art professor, George, helps me mat it up, then puts it under acetate or shrink-wrap. The shrink-wrap and the mat board can be expensive, but I don't mind. And neither would you if you saw the drawings when they were done – all professional-looking and framed like someone thought they were worth preserving. Only I don't have any place to put them. I just stack them under the bed because they're too heavy to hang on the walls.

Remember what I used to paint besides castles near the water? I once drew women from magazines and gave them long hair flowing past their ankles. I once drew you. I gave you and the models naked, skeletal bodies. George thought I had a wonderful mind whenever he saw the figures I sketched. He thought I created them out of this vision I had whenever I took up the blank paper. Only he was wrong. I had no control over what I was drawing.

I know I'm no artist. I began by sketching healthy young women. I began by sketching you, but my drawings turned out more humanoid than human – eyes bigger than fists, arms like radio antennas, breasts bigger than heads and rounder than eyes. The drawings did have a certain charm, a starving neglect of anything on a woman that's not made for beauty.

Some nights I dream of those women. I also dream of you. I want us all to hold each other, to keep our naked bodies from shivering.

I'm not ashamed of my dreams, but I'm afraid to tell you what happened to the drawings of you, why I stopped looking you in the eye, why I stopped calling you for so long.

"What a faggot," Angel Boy said to Launa a month ago when he found my stash of magazines. "Do you think she's a lesbian? Do you think she'll marry a woman some day?"

How could I tell you what he said to me? The last time I came into his room, he lifted me up and dropped me. It was just an accident, but that night I gave up painting women. I gave up painting you and began painting the castle for our shadows to hide in.

This morning I take the castle painting to George at the college. He's quiet as I hold it up to him. When he sighs, I know there's something wrong. Apparently, the flaw is in the vision of the water.

"This looks like something you would have done when you just started out," he says.

"Well, what can I do to change it?"

"I don't know. Look at the water. That doesn't look like real water."

"How can I make it right?"

"You know how a sea looks? You've seen waves before?"

"So what should I do now?"

"It's hard to say. There's always other paintings."

So I take the canvas down to the wood shop and use the electric sander to get rid of the texture of the cheap acrylic. Then I find better paints, thicker and in tubes, much more expensive. But George paid for them, so there's no need to worry. I paint Mars Black over the entire canvas.

By noon, against my better instincts, I begin a portrait of a woman's face, her features hugely drawn. This time I don't even waste my time remembering your mouth or looking for faces in magazines. I just begin to paint, and this painting is turning out better than the other, or so George tells me.

I give the woman white hair flying out from her face as if the strands are bothered by wind. Another student asks George if the woman's irises are the globes of two worlds. I don't know. Maybe yes, maybe no. One way or the other, it really doesn't matter. If you do the wrong thing, if you ever look at the painting close up instead of from far away, you can still see the outline of the castle under the black.

My dreams are that way. They don't erase easy. Now Launa and Dupus have found a way to stop dreaming dreams. I don't blame them. It's hard to dream an ocean then have someone tell you there's no water in the waves' green water. It's hard to dream a dream without you.

Through my bedroom window, I watch Launa and Waniel go for walks beside the woods. If you were looking, you could see the lines of the hard muscles working in their legs as they go along.

Really, I don't blame them. Painting makes me tired – my body still as my eyes and the brush move over the canvas – and sleeping will make me dream of you. I usually get paint in my hair and on my jeans, and the stains don't wash out, so I'll never look flawless like one of those models in the magazines. And if I'm always painting instead of walking with Angel Boy, he'll never pick me a yellow flower.

They walk by the yellow flowers growing by a tree near the duck pond. Kissy Boy doesn't say anything. Neither does Launa. She just looks at those flowers, and he walks over there and picks the brightest one. He hands it to her. She smiles. When they get home, she puts it in a jelly jar filled with tap water and calls the flower a daffodil. It's really a jonquil. But who's going to tell her that? And what difference does it make anyway?

At six o'clock in the evening, I'm in bed when Launa knocks on the door to my room. She would never sleep like this when she wasn't tired. She'll never know the joys of basking in the sickness – at night touching women in dreams, feeling your arms on my shoulders, visiting men who would never talk to me in daylight when I have all that acrylic in my stringy, brown hair. Those men's chests are muscled like my brother's but never hairless.

142

They have filthy, springy shags of black hair sticking to their skin for no apparent reason, like camel hair dried on canvas.

In the day, I pull the sheets over my head to make it night, but first I turn on the radio. That way the moment just before I fall asleep, I'll get confused and think the songs are about us.

That's what I'm thinking when I hear Launa's knock at the door. I pull the green sheets higher over my head and crouch down under the pillow, but she and Woener come into the room anyway.

"Wake her up," Cupie says with a man's voice.

"No," she says, "you do it."

"I'm not going to touch her."

"Okay." A hand reaches out for my shoulder. "Ashley, can you hear me? Wake up."

I look out from the sheets. Launa's laughing at Bustaman and holding on to the bedpost. I'm awake now. Don't make me watch what they're doing.

Dupus takes Launa's ankle into his hand and lifts one of her suntanned legs into the air.

Kissy Boy smiles. She just looks at him. He lifts it higher. Higher.

Then he stops his arm and her leg in midair. He's scared this time he has lifted it too far.

She smiles. Smile.

"Go ahead," she says. "Lift it higher."

Wingbow lifts it higher. Smile.

"Higher," she says.

Bo Dienger pulls her leg up so high that her foot is over her head and touching the wall behind her.

Angel Boy smiles again. They're not gymnasts. He doesn't stop pushing. She doesn't cry out. He doesn't have to let go.

That's why he loves her.

THE LAST SECRET TOUR

The first summer evening Kenny searched the house, he noticed tiny beetles on the curtains where the windows had been opened for days. In the weeks that followed, the lamps burnt out to a gray powder inside the frosted bulbs. The green beetles remained, multiplied, and drifted farther into the house as freely as the warm breezes of honeysuckle air.

Almost three months since his father went away, Kenny knew the time for searching was quickly passing him by. After ransacking every cluttered room, he found nothing encouraging, not even one dark hair glistening under the beetle legs.

He was twelve years old that June, thinking the worst of what happened was not that his father had gone but that he seemed to go on leaving. With patterns of paisleys, angels, clovers, and silver stars, Kenny's mother had papered over the photographs hanging on the walls. He saw the lumps of the hidden frames swollen like wounds under the delicate paper.

Counting himself, Kenny knew of only two things his father had left behind. The second was the cat named Thaddeus. After his father went away, it refused to eat anything but live birds. By April, the cat clawed Kenny's arms while he slept, so he tried to stay awake rather than wrap himself in thick blankets during the warm nights. Finally, the cat got lost in the house.

Kenny began to notice the sweet stench of captured birds near the swing.

Today the smell was unbearable. He leaned out the open window to get away from it. Green beetle wings rumbled, flying over his hair.

The window looked out onto a narrow porch covered in tree shadow. Kenny remembered a time before sparrow tails fell sadder than dead leaves across the banisters. Thaddeus used to come running whenever his father poured cream into a teacup. His father had a habit of emptying dry cat food like wood chips into a silver bowl before dark. Thaddeus befriended Kenny then, leaping onto his shoulders when he sat down in the dinner chair. Thaddeus's eyes were as wet and dark as an oil spill catching lamplight.

Kenny thought he had been alone in the house all day, so he was surprised to see his neighbor, Mr. Shemise, walking between the faded porch columns. With a long broom, Shemise began sweeping the porch, stirring mists of dust, uncovering layers of autumn leaves, singing a brisk song about the railroad.

"Why are you sweeping our porch?" Kenny called out the open window.

"A neighbor has to do his duty. Your mother needs all the help she can take, what with all the trouble lately." He moved the broom in slanting strokes, flinging clouds of filth into the high winds blowing over the roof.

"It's too hot and you're too old to be out in this heat. Mother wouldn't want you here."

"Maybe you're right," Shemise said, turning the broom

over to dislodge a mud-dauber nest. "But your mother is still a beautiful lady, and you're a fine young man. Much too fine to be living alone in filth like this. I'll admit I'm old, but not too old to lend a hand to you both."

"She'll be angry." Kenny flicked a bright beetle off his shoulder.

"I saw that," Mr. Shemise shouted. "You've got an infestation in there. Crickets? Flies? Roaches, I'll rid you of them, too."

Kenny ducked back inside, beginning the search all over again on another secret tour of the sprawling house. From the outside, the house remained as it was when his father lived there. On the inside, the space to walk through kept getting smaller.

In the mornings, his mother went off to estate sales and in the evenings drove her pickup back, the bed loaded down with furniture, paintings, crystal figurines, and devices that had outlasted the purposes they were made for a lifetime ago.

What she bought smelled of other peoples' cats, cigars, laundry, and children. Inside her house, these different odors mingled until Kenny could no longer smell his father's after-shave or even his mother's perfume.

Just to walk through the house, he had to get on the right paths. He crawled over disintegrating couches and the hard backs of high chairs. He slid over a table that spanned the length of the dining room. Then he climbed onto the top of a china hutch to get a view of the kitchen and the living room.

"Thaddeus? Thaddeus," he called out, but he heard only the wind howling through the chimneys.

On his perch, he found a blank greeting card, a black-and-white photo of a woman he had never seen before, the arm of a doll, and his father's glasses. Kenny felt one of his shoes slipping. He almost fell off the hutch. The glasses were the first thing his father had reached for in the mornings. They weren't just for reading but for seeing objects far away. Kenny put the glasses into his shirt pocket before he jumped down, imagining how dim the dazzling leaves swaying over the summer streets were to his father without them.

A record skipped on the player in the bedroom where his mother sat on a cushioned chair, her hair falling over her face as she flipped through an oversized magazine. Kenny walked quietly into the room. In the magazine she held and in the ones all around her feet were no words or human figures, only photos of large houses filled with rare furniture.

"Honey, what now?" she asked, never glancing up from her magazine. "Can't you see I'm looking at my pictures?"

He was thinking she had been beautiful all her life up to now. From a distance, she was still lovely, but in a frenzied fashion that made her appear slightly damaged. She had a starved look of lazy hunger, like an animal awakening from a long hibernation. Her hair was caught in a frazzled mess of tangled string and frayed ribbon.

"I'll leave you alone," Kenny said. "I was just looking for

Thaddeus."

"Good."

"I'll leave you alone if you tell me what happened to my dad." Kenny put his hand in his shirt pocket and delicately touched the glasses.

"He's not here, honey." She turned the page. "Not coming back."

"Why?" He began to pull the glasses out of his pocket. He wondered what she would say if she saw them.

"It's not worth telling."

"No. What really happened? Tell me about the fight."

"There was no fight." She looked at him sadly.

"What about the trouble?" He slipped the glasses back into his shirt pocket, hoping she hadn't seen.

"What trouble?"

He let his gaze wander over the bedroom to see how it had changed. Tiny rocking chairs toppled over onto footstools and metal lanterns. A breeze riffled through the curtains, and green beetles were blown into empty candlesticks and a vase of preserved flowers. An antique bathtub supported by four metal claws sat in the center of the room where the bed used to be.

The bathtub was not used for ordinary purposes. From the sight of the tangles in his mother's hair, Kenny supposed she had given up on bathing long ago. Where a tub would usually be filled with water, this one was full of blankets, and where there should have been bubbles clinging to the sides, round beetles skittered over the old porcelain.

Waking the next morning, Kenny began to reach for his father's glasses but was startled by the gaunt figure of Mr. Shemise leaning into his bedroom window. His hair was as wispy and disheveled as a branch dangling scorched leaves. His teeth released a jagged shine like broken shells littering the lakeshore.

"Good morning," Mr. Shemise called in the open window.

The old man lifted one long leg over the windowsill. When Kenny saw the shadow of Shemise's big shoes falling over the carpet, he put on the glasses, and the room became a blur of muted colors.

"That's a window, not a door," Kenny said, stepping out of bed. "Come to the front, and I'll let you in that way."

"Nice spectacles," Shemise said.

Kenny ran to the door. Its wood had swollen from the heat. He had to tug the knob several times to loosen it from the frame.

Shemise stepped into the house after stamping his shoes on the rug. "I plan to fix that door with some soap and oil," he said. "But first I'll have a word with your mother."

"She's sleeping." Kenny removed the glasses, slipping them into his shirt pocket.

"Not feeling well, is she? I'll bet my big toe it isn't catching. Let me check on her just the same."

Shemise stood still before the open door of her bedroom. Waiting behind the old man, Kenny could see his mother's long, dingy hair spilling out of the old tub. Stepping gingerly into the

150

bedroom, Mr. Shemise whispered that a bathtub was a charming place for a woman to sleep. She was propped up on couch pillows. A light sheet hung over her shoulders. Her eyelids were almost glistening. Kenny saw the hairlines of the cat scratches long faded on her arms.

Shemise put one hand across her neck as if to check her pulse. Kenny also leaned over her, listening for the breath slipping through her soft mouth. He thought she spoke his father's name before opening her eyes.

She sat up, knocking her head hard against the chipped porcelain. "You dirty old fool," she said. "Get out of my room. What do you want with me? Get out!"

Kenny followed Mr. Shemise to the place at the end of the shadowed hallway where the loose porch swing was propped up against the walls, painted chains trailing off into the darkness of the corner behind it. The candied odor grew almost syrupy near the swing. Kenny thought the lost cat had crawled into the space between the walls to hide there, still secretly feeding on the sparrows that nested in the chimneys. He realized how badly Mr. Shemise wanted to stay inside his mother's house by the way the old man took in the honeyed drafts from the wounded birds, a single jerk of the head and shoulders, then a gradual stiffening into a rigid posture as he collected himself, saying, "Forgive me. I had a sudden spasm in my leg."

When Kenny's mother stepped out of her room, she knocked a painted hummingbird feeder off a cherry-wood table.

The tip of her shoe grazed the handle of a glass bell, which lay in a clutter of perfume bottles on the floor. She walked through the hallway while the bell rolled past Kenny and into the chains of the broken swing. He heard the clapper knocking against the sides before the bell finally hit the wall and Mr. Shemise went down on his knees to pick up a piece of the fractured handle.

A ray of light coming from a window beyond the hallway glanced off the handle as the old man offered Kenny's mother the broken piece. She stopped in front of him to examine it with just the tips of her fingers. She raised her eyebrows in confusion, but with one look at Mr. Shemise, she tossed the handle into the space behind the swing and sighed. After sweeping a strand of Kenny's hair away from his eyes, she continued toward the light at the end of the hallway. Then she paused for a moment, her delicate body twisting as she looked back, her hair shrouded in the dusty light, her lips moving as surely as a child's laughing at a very old man.

"There is a big auction I'm off to," she said. "That and a few estate sales, a yard sale some friends are putting on, and a flea market I haven't been to in ages."

"When can the boy expect you back?" Shemise asked.

"Don't worry. I won't buy much. I'm not really looking today."

"I'll be fine, Mom. Shemise was just leaving," said Kenny.

"I was. But before I go, if you don't mind my saying . . ."

"Mr. Shemise," she said as she clamped her purse with a loud snap, "I'm really in a hurry."

"Well, I was just saying to the boy –" his gaze moved over the dusty mirrors, the broken swing, the scattered perfume bottles, the oversized wardrobe with its gaping drawers " – I don't know how his father could stand to leave all that he did."

She sighed, calming Kenny with the long, careful sound of her wordless voice. "I know. I've always thought this house was something special." She straightened a clock on the wall, and with a flick of her long finger put the pendulum back into motion. "Still is."

"I was just on my way out. Allow me to walk you," Shemise said. He hurried to her side, his hands never leaving the papered walls until the last moment.

The door opened and closed, and the lock clicked into place.

Kenny examined his father's glasses, unfolded them, and slipped them on in silence. He searched the fireplaces for Thaddeus. But behind the glasses, Kenny's vision was so hazy all he saw was a dark slur of charred rubble.

His mother came back in the late evening with a pickup full of dolls, wineglasses, and white, painted rocking chairs toppled over onto their sides. She also brought the tiniest man Kenny had ever seen, and she called him Russell. When she introduced him, Kenny thought he might be frail. But when Russell began to carry the rocking chairs, one in each hand, and the crates of wineglasses under his arms, Kenny realized that what he mistook for frailty was actually the extraordinary sleekness of a man who was more muscle than skin or bone. He was tiny, but he was so compact that it would have been impossible to carry his body like that of a child.

Kenny's mother held a porcelain doll missing an arm and part of a foot. She was already talking about buying miniature, black patent shoes.

"Russell, do you think we could find shoes to fit such tiny feet?" she asked with an urgency in her voice that Kenny hadn't heard since the February evenings his father walked his bicycle up the porch steps. Kenny felt the glasses pop like tiny bones shifting inside his pocket as he moved.

"I suppose a person could find just about anything if she looked hard enough," Russell said. He began to whistle as his gaze traveled over the candlesticks, the tabletops covered with lamps of all sizes, the cushioned chairs backed up to the walls, the leather-bound journals stacked to the ceiling.

"Our cat has been missing for a long time," she said, fluttering her eyelids in Russell's direction.

Kenny thought Russell looked like a young banker in a black-and-white photo of the Old West. Not long ago, Kenny's mother had begun collecting such photos to hang in her bedroom. Russell wore a striped suit with a gold watch chain dangling from the breast pocket. He had dark, glistening eyes the color of his mustache, which looked as if it were drawn on with a pencil. As he touched his mustache, his face took on a sullen expression.

"Why don't we try something different for dinner?" Kenny's mother asked as she placed a plate of white cookies and a bowl of strawberry jam on one end of the long table. "Russell claims this is all he ever eats anymore. Why, I don't know what we're going to do with him. I guess he takes some getting used to."

"Thanks, Mrs. Kendall," Russell said as he sat down to his plate of cookies.

"Now, stop that nonsense. I feel younger than I ever did."

"What nonsense?" he asked, devouring a cookie.

"Nothing. Just being around all these things that were new when I was a little girl is almost enough to make me feel younger, like I've gone back to a long time ago."

"Now that's nonsense, Lee Anne," he said, laughing as he reached for her hand and took it to his lips like he would a white cookie.

She squealed with delight and said, "Tell Kenny how you're going to solve our problem."

"What has your kid got in his shirt pocket? He keeps sticking his fingers in his pocket."

"So what? Tell him what you do," she said, giving Kenny a knowing wink.

"I," he said, turning to Kenny, "am a crawler. I go through the ruins of buildings and get into spaces where most people would never go. Most would be afraid once they got in there they would never come out. Some don't."

"I don't understand anything he says, Mom." Kenny dipped a cookie into the red jam.

"I can go through ventilation systems, tunnels, and under collapsed roofs. Behind walls, Kenny. You would be surprised what you can find there."

"I think I'd be disappointed. I wouldn't want to go in

those places. They would just be dark and full of dead stuff, roaches," Kenny said as he licked the crumbs off his fingers.

"Yes, and lost valuables, things that have been misplaced and haven't been seen in years. Things people would pay to see again."

"You'll find that cat for us, won't you, honey?" Kenny's mother asked Russell.

"I'm not done talking to the boy," Russell said. He reached for another cookie and began to spoon on the jam. "When I was your age, I was still the smallest of my brothers – the one who had to crawl inside the tractor to work on the engine while the tractor was still running. Because I'm small and have small hands, I can do things others can't. You'll see how it works to my advantage."

He rose from the table abruptly and started off in the direction of the hallway. He ran his hands over the intricate patterns of the wallpaper Kenny's mother had recovered at least a dozen times since his father left.

"Lee Anne, get a hammer," Russell shouted to Kenny's mother.

She came back with a medium-sized hammer. With the sharp, curved end, Russell pounded out a space in the wall the circumference of a large woman's hat or an opened parasol. Then he dropped the hammer behind the swing, took off his jacket and shirt, and reached into the hole with one arm.

"I need at least one of you to wait out here just to be sure I can get myself back out," he said. He put his whole head inside the wall as if he were just looking. Then he turned his body away from them and pulled his other arm inside. He twisted his back so that even his legs were taken in and just his shoes were left hanging out of the wall.

"I've got something," he said, his voice muffled. "Now pull me out."

Kenny looked at his mother in disbelief. Her fingers were working nervously in her long hair to loosen the tangles as she stared at the soles of Russell's shoes. Kenny grabbed a shoe in each hand and leaned back with all his weight. Russell's body slowly emerged from inside the wall – his trousers covered with lint, his hairless chest and arms dotted with blood as if he had fallen into a vat of needles, his hair heaped in white debris. His hands were holding gray fur, jumbled bones, and a cat skull in which two sockets for lost eyes gaped out in the direction of light beyond the hallway.

"I guess I got caught on a board," Russell said. "Lord knows what else you've got back there." He studied the cat's body as if he didn't know where to put it.

"Lord knows," Kenny's mother said, sitting down on the swing.

"What happened to its eyes?" asked Kenny.

"Oh, anything," Russell said. "You didn't always live in this house?"

"No. It's very old. We were going to restore it," she said.

"Before we fix the old place up, she might be worth a look."

Kenny held a plastic bag out to Russell. "Put the cat in here."

"Not so fast," Russell said as he pulled the cat closer to his chest and stroked its fur until single hairs fell off onto the carpet. "Tell me its name."

"I don't remember."

"Thaddeus," Kenny's mother said. Russell dropped the cat into the plastic bag.

The doorbell chimed. "It's probably Shemise," Kenny said.

His mother reached for the cat bag. "For once that old man will make himself useful." She and Kenny went to the door while she called back to Russell, "Just stay where you are."

Mr. Shemise looked in through the window and waved. Kenny's mother unlocked the door.

"Good night, Mr. Shemise," she said.

"Just passing through and thought to say hello. Is there any way I can be of service?"

Mr. Shemise took the plastic bag with a humble smile. For the first time since his father went away, Kenny felt sorry for the old man, knowing he could not resist looking inside. Shemise opened the bag and closed it quickly. For a single moment, he shut his eyes, then gave Kenny's mother a sympathetic nod. "I'll take care of this right away," he said.

Kenny followed Shemise into the backyard. He couldn't stand to see the worn expression on Shemise's face, so he put on his father's glasses to dim the signs of the old man's suffering.

Shemise dug a perfectly rectangular plot, all along forcing the shovel down into the earth with extreme slowness.

"I know what this cat must have meant to your mother," he said, as he struggled with the hard earth without ever slouching over, as if he took pride in the digging. By the time he had filled the hole, it was dark out. Through the thick lenses, Kenny could barely see the trees through the roof's shadow.

"I notice there is no light coming from your windows," Shemise said, shaking his head at the house.

"Bulb's burnt out," said Kenny. He remembered his father standing on a ladder, unscrewing the dusty globes of the high lamps.

"Remind me to replace them tomorrow." Shemise started off in the direction of his own house. "Let me know if you ever need anything. You know where to reach me."

Inside the dark house, Russell smoked a fat cigar and fell asleep in the swing. The fire on the tip that flared as he breathed was the only warm light inside. Through the windows came the harsh light of the moon, too stark to do anything but cast shadows. While Russell lulled himself to sleep in the wicker swing tottering like a giant cradle, he seemed to Kenny to be more of a child than a man. The longer Kenny looked at him the more he felt afraid for himself and his mother.

When Kenny woke up in the hallway full of cigar smoke, he thought the house had finally caught fire. He put a hand in his shirt pocket to secure his father's glasses in the midst of the heat and destruction he waited for. But there were no flames, and Russell was nowhere in sight. The sun had risen, and Kenny could see the beetles again. He walked carefully into his mother's bedroom. He did not disturb a single perfume bottle.

Inside the porcelain tub, Russell and Kenny's mother were asleep and glistening with moisture, their hair wet with perspiration. With beetles crawling over their skin, they looked like a drowned mother and her child. Kenny felt like he had to be the one to walk in and pull the plug.

Russell stepped out of the tub in two graceful movements, then slid into his trousers.

"Your mustache is coming off," Kenny said.

"Oh, God," Russell said, running off to a room with better light and a decent mirror. When they were far enough away from Kenny's mother, Russell sighed and with a single swipe of his wrist smeared the mustache off his lip. He looked at Kenny with undisguised contempt, reached into his trouser pocket, and pulled out a brown makeup pencil.

"How old are you really?" Kenny asked, stepping behind Russell so he could watch them both in the mirror.

"Twenty-three in December," Russell said, beginning to draw the hairs back in.

Kenny put on his father's glasses to give him courage. "Like hell you are," he said.

"Better watch what you say to me, kid," Russell said, his voice deep but almost wavering. "Those glasses make you look like a disaster, an idiot."

Kenny removed the glasses and saw Russell's dark eyes

glittering in the reflection.

"Tell anyone what you just saw, and I'll kill us both," Russell said. He took down the mirror and turned it on its side. "Your mother makes three."

Now dressed in blue velvet, Kenny's mother stepped into the room. "I'm off to another sale," she said before giving them each a kiss.

"I guess I had better get to work," Russell said.

"Do your worst." Even with her high heels on, she skipped out into the cluttered hallway.

Kenny heard the pickup start once before the engine died and began to run again. Recognizing the even sound of the tires rolling, he picked up the earpiece of an old-fashioned wall phone and held it against the side of his head. He caught a whiff of his father's hair tonic on the dark cord and stood still for a long time just to breathe it in. When he finally let the cord drop, the seven numbers he dialed spun like time on a fast watch.

He heard the blunt sounds of steady destruction, Russell's exploration of the narrow spaces hidden between the walls. Kenny swallowed hard. From his mother's bedroom came a pounding that shook the entire house.

"Shemise," Kenny said into the mouthpiece, "get over here right away."

The old man let himself in through the front door. He held a small creature in his hands. Kenny could not yet see what it was. The way it wriggled, he thought it might be a crippled squirrel or a young raccoon taken from the wild.

"How are things holding up around here?" Shemise asked, moving toward the source of the pounding. He handed Kenny a tiny, silver kitten with yellow eyes. "I thought this critter might amuse your mother."

"Mother has found someone," Kenny said. He dropped the kitten on a cushioned chair. It jumped down and began to explore the house in slow steps, twitching, taking a little freedom with a little terror.

The hammering stopped.

"A woman who loves so many old things shouldn't mind having an old man around," Shemise said with a humble gaze cast down to the carpet.

"You don't understand. He's my age, a child."

Shemise fingered a lump under the wallpaper. "I had hoped things would turn out differently," he said. "But for the time being, I'll have to let your mother come to her own conclusions."

They went into her bedroom where one wall had been hammered open. Sunlight cast the shadows of the wires into the shape of trailing hair.

"He's in here somewhere," Kenny said, as he knocked on the wall.

"Over here," Russell shouted, slipping out from a narrow space behind the oak wardrobe. He was dangling the kitten by its tail while it trembled silkily like a live fish taken out of the water.

"Good to meet you," Mr. Shemise said to Russell, who was covered in white dust.

"Don't you notice anything strange?" Kenny whispered into Mr. Shemise's closer ear.

"Well, he's holding the kitten by the tail, and the renovation has finally begun. When your father lived here, I never thought I'd live to see the day," the old man said with a final click of his tongue.

"I'll get back to work," Russell said, releasing the kitten before he slipped back behind the wardrobe.

A wistful smile surfaced as the wrinkles shifted on Shemise's hollow face.

"What am I going to do?" Kenny asked. The kitten traipsed over his feet. When he reached down to stroke it, it cowered away from him.

"I'll just stick around in any case," Shemise said with a small laugh that grew raw as it trailed off. "You may not believe me now, but we're lucky the renovation has finally begun. I always thought some day this place would fall to rubble. Now I know it will be resurrected. You may be unhappy now, but people learn to understand luck in different ways."

Kenny felt his father's glasses pressing through his shirt pocket near his chest. They remained as delicate and forbidding as shattered glass, broken claws, and fractured bones. He wanted his mother to touch them, to hold them in her hands and tell him how they came to rest, lost or abandoned, on top of the china hutch.

Kenny heard the pickup pull into the driveway. A moment later, his mother walked into the room triumphantly in her rumpled, blue-velvet gown. She held a glass sphere filled with moss and dead butterflies.

The old man blew her a single kiss, blue veins rippling like ribbons untangling under the clear skin of his arms. But she made no gesture to take it from the air. Instead, she put the globe on the table where the hummingbird feeder used to sit. "She really is looking younger," Shemise said, "but that's happiness for you. It can disguise even the years."

Russell stepped out from behind the wardrobe to greet her. "Any luck?" she asked, pushing the kitten away from her with her scuffed shoes, the pointed heels coming close to its eyes.

"I only found this," Russell said as he handed her a frayed, brown wallet.

"Where?" Kenny asked.

"Behind the wardrobe."

Kenny took the wallet from Russell's hands. "Did you know it was there?" he asked his mother. "And I found these." Kenny put his hand into his shirt pocket and pulled out his father's glasses. He noticed the lenses were cracked and the frames bent.

"Put those away," his mother said. She took the glasses from him and flung them at the kitten where it crouched next to an ivory comb under the antique tub.

Kenny ran out into the hallway and stopped where the wall gaped open over the swing. With his hands on the wall that remained, he examined the heavy lumps of the photographs behind the paper. He began to tear the layers away: a blue layer, a yellow, a teal, a green, another blue . . . until he recognized the old colors. Still hanging in its familiar place was a photo of himself and his father standing in front of the house a long time ago; not far away, his mother with her face in her hands, looking out from her fingers with the expression of a small girl who thinks she can hide herself by covering only her eyes. A photo of Thaddeus walking the roof. A photo of his father sailing a white boat on the open ocean.

BARONESS WITH STRANGE EYES

Texas in springtime, long lines of cars lace the highway.
Downtown, pickup trucks full of long-haired girls pass shops
selling big earrings and white hats. Mother hums behind the
wheel of her shabby car. She drives me places I never wanted to
go. On the strange side of Houston, an old tattoo parlor thrives on
the fringe. Mother parks the car and rushes to the parlor's door. I
follow her wherever she goes, even though we're too old for this
now.

Inside the parlor, I feel panic setting in like a slow sickness
defining itself in familiar symptoms – chills, shortness of breath,
dizzy spells. In the dim room, it's hard to read Mother's face. I
can't decide what she's capable of understanding.

Maybe the parlor's gaudy collection of photos will be my
undoing. A strange girl like me can't compete with walls covered
in photos of beautiful women. Their legs are adorned with etched
designs, sleeping tigers, mermaids, moons, twin dragonflies,
winged girls, and swords. Their arms are tattooed with winding
chains, entangled vines, and blue ivy drifts. Other photos show
women in black-suede cowboy hats. Old and young, all are
smiling, pulling back their sleeves or skirts to reveal personalized
tattoos – a red monarch soaring over the name ANNA, SAM etched
in fire, BABY tattooed under a sleeping panther, an indigo unicorn

166

blazing a trail that reads MEGAN.

I stand near an ancient black-and-white photo, charred and dated 1932, hanging among the rest without an explanation for its age. BARONESS C. its caption reads. In the photo, a dark-haired woman reclines with a girl in her arms. Both are wearing the same type of dress, ruffles and satin. The woman is lifting the edge of the girl's dress to reveal a tattoo of a sphinx. Like the girl, the woman has large eyes painted Texas-style with long lashes and lots of dark makeup. "Debutantes," I whisper to Mother.

Considering a tattoo of a sphinx for my own leg, I want Mother and me to be like Baroness C. and her child, a perfect fit with the women on the wall. I turn toward Mother to see if she has noticed the photo. She studies books of calligraphy, letters flowing under her hand's shadow. Just when I'm about to tell her I want the sphinx etched into my leg, I change my mind. Texas is no place for an odd tattooed girl, ugly enough to stand out in crowds.

A swoop, a clatter of footsteps, and a woman with no hair walks out from the curtained doorway. Her naked head gleams under the globe lights. She rustles the faded fabric that swipes her scrawny arms. I recognize her from her photo in the newspaper, the infamous tattooist who owns the parlor and lives in the rooms above. Once an unruly debutante, she ruined herself with her own needle. I remember the outrageous rumors of her as a young girl, refusing to court old money. She used to advertise by undressing at cocktail parties decades ago. She had so many tattoos that there wasn't a single patch of unmarred skin on her tiny body.

Because the tattooist is bald, she's no woman at all to me. Big hair is important to Texas women. Fragile and shapely, susceptible to chemicals, razors, and fire, hair can ruin a woman by putting a lovely face in an ugly frame. It can hide a sad face like mine behind long, straight strands. The tattooist approaches me with her palms open, raising her hands as if to touch my bangs. I step away from her and stand behind Mother, who turns around as if warning me not to embarrass her.

"Don't be shy," the tattooist says loudly. Her huge smile exposes silver-capped teeth. I try not to stare at her head, try not to imagine what could be more shocking than a tattooed woman with no hair. She's everything I'm afraid of becoming, everything except fat. Because she's very thin, I envy her despite her baldness. With her narrow hips, she's skinner than I am. I like to be the thinnest woman in the room wherever I go. If I am the skinniest, then I'm the best, no matter who the others are, no matter what accomplishments – lovely children, pretty faces, sexy husbands, glamorous jobs, perfectly rounded breasts – other women might try to hold against me.

Taking a closer look, I can't tell what age the tattooist is. She could be ninety-six or sixty-nine. She's a woman, I think, who has wounded herself regularly and with more intensity than she'll ever hurt my mother or me.

Tiny jewels flash on the tips of her eyelashes, blue and spiked like the legs of a tropical spider bathed in dew. Her eyebrows have been plucked away and inked back in with a needle. Her hair is the same way: gone, the bare skin drawn over with care, the outline of every missing curl traced past her neckline. As she leans over Mother, I see the permanent shadow, tresses etched into the valley between her breasts.

"That's me," the tattooist says, her head drooping shyly.

"What?" I ask, not sure she's talking to me.

"Baroness C. was my mother," she says, pointing to the photo of the baroness and child. I want to ask her how much she weighs, how much she has eaten today just to be sure I've eaten less. I want to ask why she shaved off all her hair just to clear the canvas of her skin. I wonder if the tattoos are worth it.

"How did you do that to your eyelashes?" I ask instead. I sit down and begin to swivel in the barber chair next to Mother, who turns away from me and removes her shirt. Wearing only blue jeans and a lace bra, she stretches out on the low table.

"Hush, honey," Mother says without opening her eyes. "The lady needs to concentrate."

"It's a secret," the tattooist says, the live needle hovering over Mother's smooth shoulder, "but I can show you for nineteen-fifty."

"Anyone can do that," I say, "with a little glue and black paint."

"Think again," she says, the needle beginning to quiver. "What if you lose the jewels in your eyes?"

I wonder if Mother will suddenly open her eyes, look at the tattooist's face, and be frightened by her strangeness. But Mother keeps her eyes shut the entire time the needle hums on, slowly moving toward her.

Mother and I have waited a long time for this – days imagining tattoos on our arms and shoulders where there once were only dark impressions from the sun, hours spent in jade-tinged rooms lingering over Celtic designs, drawings of ships and orchids, panthers, astrological signs, blue human eyes, photos of exotic frogs.

"Shit," Mother says as the needle touches down on her shoulder. Then she's quiet. Her slight body falls into stillness. Her eyes grow strange under the shadow of the tattooist's hands moving over her.

I'm afraid for Mother when she begins to groan soft and low and shameless like a child under the buzzing needle. Turning away, I look at my own reflection. I'm wearing white jeans and a blue sweater that once belonged to Mother during her college years. Its style and color are so ordinary it can't be easily recognized as a sweater from a long time ago. Occasionally, when no one else is watching, I gaze through the tiny holes in the weave. The edges of my bra vanish into the pale skin that shows through.

Mother looks young as I compare her reflection with mine. Her light hair frames her smooth face. My hair is dull and stringy, shadowing my narrow eyes. Mother's eyes, accented with velvety makeup, are luminous light-catchers. She smiles when she sees me looking at her. I don't smile back.

I'm too busy frowning at my own reflection, the grayish, gaunt face where the cheekbones protrude under sunken eyes, making twin shadow-hollows on either side of my long nose. Because I've lost so much weight so quickly, I have the face of an old woman. I look much older than Mother, even though I still feel like a child. I can see the vague outline of my teeth just above my lip even though my mouth is closed. But my greatest wish is that I was thinner.

There's one secret not even Mother knows: I imagine myself as a young girl with nervous, glittering eyes and small, hairless legs. Over the years, my eyes have changed little. They're still suspicious-seeming, veiled by dark lashes. My legs are another story. Because they've grown long and hairy, no one except Mother calls me little Zale anymore.

Sometimes I refuse to go to sleep at night and to eat my lunch and dinner. Texas is no place for a fat girl, so I hide in my room. Sometimes I vomit in the plastic bag I leave under my bed. Every night, I imagine acid eats away at the clear seams. The bag dissolves, slowly ripping apart.

Instead of bread rising in the oven, I'm drawn to mirrors, windows, and Mother's blue and yellow birds twitching in their cages.

Not even Mother knows what it's like for me walking from one mirror to another, searching for the perfect little Zale I want to be, never finding her in my reflection. Whenever I'm alone, I undress in front of the long mirror in my room and confirm my darkest suspicions. My breasts are gone. I watch my ribs and pelvic bones surface and recede as I hunch and flail, twisting my arms and legs, turning my head, holding a tiny hand mirror up to the long mirror so that I can see my naked body from every position imaginable. Scrutinizing my thighs and stomach, I cup the small weight of my hips in my hands and chastise myself for what food I've eaten.

Sometimes in the locked study, Mother turns off all the lights so I can't see my reflection in the dark window. She asks me what I see in the mirrors, but I'm afraid to tell her my nipples and belly are covered with curly, black hairs. Texas is no place for a hairy girl, so in the evenings, I pluck the hairs off my breasts with tiny, silver tweezers and flush the hairs down the toilet.

I've starved myself for so long I no longer hunger. At night, Mother whispers women's secrets – how I can stay alive with the help of vitamin pills, how I can apply white makeup to my face to make myself seem young again. The old fear still haunts us. Even now, Mother thinks I'm growing old before my time. I still think I'm fat for my age.

At night, although the mirrors go dark, there is no peace for us in our house. From the locked study, the nervous, tittering birds still mock us with Father's words, saying *Don't shut me out, do I deserve this, what have I done.*

When Father left without warning, the birds held on to the sound of his voice. The house on Spencer Street still echoes with his words so that some nights Mother and I, listening to our music, often forget the house is just our own.

Father's name was Sheldon. The birds' names are Olive and Boobie. I don't know the tattooist's name, nor do I have the courage to ask her as her gaze suddenly meets mine.

Her name doesn't matter to me. I measure her the way I measure myself, arm by frail arm, watching bones rise out of skin. Only Father knew me as I really am, the way I see myself with other women, flesh and bones, eaters and shitters, virgins and whores.

In the early morning hours, I used to hear him in the study, talking to the birds, telling Olive and Boobie what he didn't have the courage to say to Mother and me. *I know you*, the birds sometimes say.

Texas is no place for a man to go insane, so Father left for Oklahoma. Now that he's gone, I'm the one who sits with the birds in the night. Boobie and Olive seem lonely without him. Mother and I still call them blue and yellow although they are really purple, teal, and gray. Their naked flesh is wrinkled and bruised where they have plucked their own feathers away.

Sometimes during the night, I take Olive out of the cage and hold her. She has taken to me in the same way Boobie has taken to Mother. Her sensitive skin bristles under my fingertips. I always think if I hold her long enough her feathers will eventually grow back. But she only falls asleep in my hand.

"You don't like me much, do you?" the tattooist asks, putting the needle down. She pinches her fingers together as if plucking an invisible hair from her eyebrow, then motions to me with a swoop of her arm to come closer. I stay where I am, my hand on Mother's elbow.

I look at Mother. She ignores me and continues to blot her

shoulder with a towel. Her hair is damp and tangled and tied into a precarious knot. When she finally meets my gaze, her eyes are full of sympathy, as if she already knows I don't want to go with the tattooist.

The tattooist nods to me, then walks away. Pulling back the curtain over the doorway, she pauses on the first step of the small, foot-worn stairway. She turns around to me, smiling sadly. I wonder if Mother has told her Father is gone.

"Is there something the matter?" Mother asks, her voice tired but gentle.

"I have something to show her," the tattooist says. "She can come upstairs with me to get you some water."

"All right," Mother says, frowning at her reflection, although she obviously likes what she sees. Her tattoo is written in perfectly formed, delicate letters that spell out COWBOYS under her messy hair. "If she wants to."

"I don't know," I say. I turn around to look at the window, hoping the tattooist will go on without me. Mother is quiet for a long time. I think by the time I turn around the tattooist will be gone. But when I look away from the birches and the slow traffic outside, she's watching me from the foot of the stairs.

"I'm coming," I say, feeling a little ridiculous. The birds, I think, are probably getting hungry. Even if we are able to get home for their normal feeding hour, there will be no time for me to get a tattoo of my own.

*   *   *

174

Staircases, after glass doors and the sound of Mother's voice fading into opera records, are my favorite things. There are no staircases in our house on Spencer Street, only the locked study with its high windows and the ladder Father used to climb to coax the birds down from the upper shelves.

The birds will live to be at least eighty years old, we were told by the pet-shop owners when we bought them six years ago. We took them home when they were just babies, days after their hatching when they were taken from their mother. The birds' lives are just beginning. They'll outlive Mother. They'll outlive Father. They might even outlive me. Eighty years is a long time for a bird to live in a study with high windows, all along using its beak to pluck away the feathers and then the sensitive skin and then the scabs off its own body. If birds are neglected, they will go insane and begin to eat themselves alive.

Upstairs, in her narrow kitchen, the tattooist drops ice cubes into a clean glass and carefully pours water from a blue pitcher over the ice. The rooms are painted rose and the floors are made of sea-foam tiles. The walls are covered in handsome still lifes of flowers and wine bottles. Postcards from Italy are fanned out around a glass clock on a cherry-wood table.

"I was once a good-looking girl like you," she tells me, smiling to reveal four silver teeth. I try to smile back at her. I know I'm not a good-looking girl but a strange girl with nervous eyes and hairy thighs. I hate my legs and look down at my shoes even as I take the glass from her hand. The ice cubes hiss and rattle as they dissolve. The glass is cool against my palm, calming me.

First I sip the water. Then I take larger swallows, even though I'm not very thirsty. The tattooist's eyes, peering out of the jewels and heavy makeup, look aware and honest. I feel like she knows many secrets that only I would know about myself – my starved body, the vacant texture of my loose-hanging skin, the lazy slump of my back, the way my legs look in a short skirt, like a boy's.

I imagine hiding my legs under a long billowing skirt for years, having tattoos etched all across my thighs. I imagine the man I would reveal my legs to – someone with dark hair, a mustache, and eyes I can't see in the shadows.

The tattooist smiles at me. "I wasn't like most women," she whispers. "You realize that by now, and you hate me for it. I can see it in your eyes."

"No, I don't," I say, feeling sad but also a little hysterical.

She refills my glass with water. Turning my back to her, I look out the upstairs window into the window of another apartment in the next building. I see a fan. Behind the blades, I concentrate on the dark forms of two children facing a television. I smell river birches and try to concentrate on the barely audible rustling of their leaves. I don't know why the tattooist has invited me into her private rooms or why I'm afraid of what she might tell me.

For a moment, there is blessed silence inside the small apartment. The tattooist walks into another room and closes the door. I think about sneaking away from her, down the musty stairway. But I stay where I am, confused and ashamed of my fear, not knowing how I would explain myself if I were caught slipping away.

When the tattooist opens the door, she is wearing only a worn black-velvet robe. Her feet and ankles are etched with purple vines that coil from her ankles to her thin, veined legs. The faces and eyes of exotic creatures – white lions, pumas, gazelles, dragonflies, diamondbacks, pale, mythic girls, and even the old sphinx – look out from the leaves.

She doesn't say anything to me. Instead, she lightly brushes her fingertips over the jewels pasted onto her eyelashes. Then she lowers her hands. Swiftly, she unties the cords of her robe and wriggles her shoulders so that the velvet falls in a dark puddle around her feet.

"There," she keeps saying, "there," as if she were trying to prove a point.

Before I realize what I've done, I spill the water from my glass. The carpet grows dark and cool at my feet. I drop the empty glass, and it rolls along the fringed rug, bumping table legs.

At first, all I see is the strange shape of her naked body, which is oddly familiar to me. Her body shows her old age, which not even her hundreds of tattoos can disguise. The tattoos are deformed by her aged skin, images drooping and sagging, blurring into each other so I can't tell what they're supposed to look like, young faces grown old, hands turning into gnarled wood, animals only dark puddles, drunken eyes.

I think of all the shapes a woman's body can take on. Fat women are often round, top-heavy, or pear-shaped, or so I've heard. Mother is an hourglass. But the tattooist and I have a different shape rarely seen or talked about in my hometown, even among women. Seeing the tattooist naked, I realize how much we're alike. Because our heads seem too big for our gaunt, stick-like bodies, we're both shaped like lollipops.

I try to find differences between my body and hers. The numerous tattoos are all I see. They begin to take on a grotesque shape. The smaller tattoos of lions and blue vines come together to form a larger pattern, transforming her small, drooping breasts into the bulging eyes of a man staring directly at me. The valley between her breasts forms his long, crooked nose. He has a face like my father's. His mouth is hidden under his beard, which is made up of the secret, dark hairs above the tattooist's legs.

"Well?" she asks. "Do you like?"

I see every rib surfacing and diving as she breathes. I open my mouth. She puts her hand over my lips, then wraps her arm around my waist and holds on. Even though I want to fight her, I cry into the bones of her shoulders.

She turns away to reach for her robe and covers herself. Before leading me down the stairs, she offers me another glass of water. Some of the water spills, splashing my feet and hands.

Downstairs the curtain is open. I can feel Mother's eyes searching mine. I'm dripping with water and beginning to shiver. Mother brushes her hair, smoothing it down over her shoulders. My hand trembles slightly, shaking the glass, spilling more water onto the floor. Mother moves her hair away from her left shoulder and examines her tattoo in the mirror.

"Will it leave a scar?" she asks.

"No," the tattooist says.

Mother takes the glass from my hand and begins to drink the remaining water quickly. "Do you still want one?" she asks, putting the glass down and looking back at her shoulder with satisfaction.

"Some other day," I say. "I'm worried about Olive."

"All right," she says, sighing.

Mother drops three crumpled bills into the tattooist's open hand. Before we leave the parlor, the tattooist takes a small black camera out of a drawer of needles.

"Smile," she says. "Now turn so we can see your tattoo. Lean in closer, put your arms around your mother. That's right," she says just after she snaps the shot.

The brightness of the flash makes white-blue shadows underneath my eyelids.

The tattooist promises to hang our photo with the other women on the wall. Mother gives her an extra ten dollars, and the tattooist tells us to take care. Mother smiles and says we will.

The rusted bell on its string clangs as I pull the handle of the glass door. The door closes behind us without another sound.

Mother lights a new cigarette in the old car, then bends backward, sucking the cigarette and trying to see the tattoo on her shoulder. As we drive away, I dip my head out the open window and see a dim profile behind the glass door of the parlor.

I try to calm myself, thinking that my skin is still pale and intact, but not for long. I wonder when I'll get a tattoo of my own, when I'll allow my body to be marred by a needle. I want a sphinx and skull, a tiny yellow daisy, a snake traveling up a slender sword, smoke, and a mermaid with long hair. I see chains and barbed wire around my wrists and ankles, a smoldering star ringing my navel, a white lion under black sky, the sun and the moon on my behind. I imagine spiders and flames, unicorns and starved panthers stalking the shadows under my arms. I want the world, the universe, everything real and imagined etched across my spine.

Even if I have to become the strangest girl in Texas, I'll take my body back one tattoo at a time. I'll create a new and perfect little Zale of my own design.

"It's all right that you didn't get one," Mother says. "I guess it takes some getting used to."

"Do you think the birds are all right?" I ask.

"The same as ever."

We drive along, our house just in sight, the roof aglow as the sun goes down. I don't want to leave Mother alone with the birds. She'll always need someone near her as she listens to her music. The records will never be enough for her. Neither will I.

Maybe Father's voice will come without warning, rising above the piano records. I don't know. Come what may, I'll never know what he was trying to tell me. And Mother will never know what the baroness's daughter and I have done to make our bodies please our eyes.

I already think of myself as a different person now. I was

so afraid when I saw myself in my mirror last night. But never again, alone in my room, my bare skin glowing bright under high lamps as the windows go dark.

COLLECTING

The wood from the carousel kit took a long time coming. While Nicky waited, Shane walked her two blocks away from his gravel yard to the house lightning had struck. All that was left on the hill was debris, the concrete foundation, and the charred, curving stairs.

The day before she had found a gold-tassel earring on the bottom step. Now she carried it in a black case. Climbing the stairs, she let the case knock against her knees so she could hear the contents rattling on the inside.

Leaning against the maple tree, Shane waved to her when she reached the top. She didn't wave back. Today was her ninth birthday, and she was waiting for her present. The week before, Shane had promised the carousel. She didn't want him to build it, would rather spend her time studying what remained of the burned house. If she listened long enough, she could hear the ashes scattering over the concrete.

She stood perfectly still for a moment to watch the bright space between his front teeth glinting like a diamond stolen from her mother's necklace. Holding the case over her head, she shook it furiously in the air. She heard a pearl bouncing over the scissors inside.

She was tired of Shane following her to the edge of the ruined house. He was twenty-nine, her father's son but too old to be her brother. He refused to climb the stairs or even set foot on the foundation. He brought along a knife to carve a circle into the maple tree.

"A pregnant lady used to live here before the big storm," Shane called up.

Nicky wasn't surprised to hear the lady was gone. Nicky's parents had also been taken by a storm while driving down the highway, but their house had survived. Shane sold it a week ago. Inside the black case, secrets of their old house remained.

When Nicky held the case close to her head and shook it, she heard the lady's tassel-chain earring drizzling into her father's shot glass inside. The day before, Nicky had found the keyhole of an old doorknob. Today, the keyhole jangled inside her case like a coin hitting the side of a fountain.

She could see birds landing on the lower housetops. A squirrel jumped onto the chimney of Shane's roof and was frightened away by a crow's circling shadow. Now that Shane was the one who took care of her, she had moved into his painted-wood house. She thought she had stayed with him for at least a month. But in his dingy neighborhood, the days passed by so slowly she couldn't be sure. Nicky looked down at her feet as the crow landed. She saw the gilded handle of a teacup. When Shane wasn't looking, she picked it up, slipping the handle into her pocket.

Nicky kept the silver latch clamped and hung the key from the gold string around her neck like a common charm. At night, she slept with the case clutched in her arms and the blanket draped over the peeling leather.

If she ever had to open the case to add to her collection, she unlatched it in the dark. She hadn't looked inside since she left the land her parents used to live on. She didn't need to. She could see everything in the case with her eyes shut just like she could still see the land unfolding on either side of the river. The sound of the keyhole clacking against her father's glasses assured her everything was still in its place.

The case had belonged to her mother, who threw it away because the red velvet on the inside was wearing back, leaving behind patches of dirty gauze. Round as the dial of the cuckoo clock at the old house, the case had once been trusted to hold her mother's famous jewelry. Now it contained items much more rare. Nicky decided to keep the contents a secret until she was a very old woman.

She never went anywhere without it. As she walked, she heard the contents rolling over the gauze: a gold screw knocking against the white top of a glass flower. In the bathroom, she laid the case beside the old tub and heard a single bead hit the blue bottle filled with water taken from the river on the land her parents used to own.

Like the soap bars in the sink, the case smelled of her mother's dresses. It once sat on top of the wardrobe in her parents' bedroom. When her mother unlocked the wardrobe doors, her skirts bellowed like carnations strewn upside-down across the floor.

Nicky scraped her fingernails on the lock and heard her mother graze the mirror with the tiny key she held between her thumb and forefinger. She remembered her mother lifting the lid of the case, the shadow of her gloved hands falling dark over the jewels.

The case had been full of gold and silver jewelry, necklaces, pendants, and pins shaped like dancers and noble insects: lady beetles, black monarchs, blue dragonflies, a praying mantis with red-bead eyes. Her mother had picked up the mantis the night of the Scygazers' cocktail party.

"Which one do you want to hold?" her mother had asked. Her parents had been dressing for the party when the summer storm rolled in with a gentle rumbling across the sky. The thunder made Nicky afraid for Canbury Green, her black horse in the barn.

"I really hate this old case," her mother had said, pouring all the jewels onto her pillow. "It's older than I am, and I'm retiring it." Nicky heard the dull thud of the case hitting the wastebasket before her mother slipped the jewelry into a velvet pouch.

Now Shane was tapping his fingers on the case as if it were a toy drum.

"I wonder whatever happened to all your mother's old jewelry," he said.

"What jewelry?" Nicky asked, pushing the case under the rug in Shane's living room.

Nicky pulled the case back toward her and spun it on its string. Inside, she heard her father's after-shave splashing in its bottle. She slapped the string hard against her thighs until it mimicked the taut sound of her mother's ballerina hair snagging on the brush. Inside the case, one of the loose mantis eyes rolled over her mother's ivory comb. Nicky heard the silver hum of the zipper on the evening dress as it glided up her mother's straight back.

"I didn't mean it that way," Shane said. "Little sister, you know I didn't."

He was drinking ice water out of a highball glass when he began talking about the carousel kit. "One hundred ninety-nine dollars in shipping fees alone. It goes from a ship to a plane to a truck on the highway." He flipped through the old carpenter's manual. "Perfect for birthday parties, big enough for all the neighborhood kids to ride on. Think of all the friends you'll have over." When he was finished with the water, swishing and swirling into his open mouth, he spat out the piece of squeezed lemon.

"My birthday was yesterday," Nicky said.

Every time a car passed by the house, he looked out the window. "You'll love it, honey. I'll bet you'll never want to ride a real horse again," he said. "How many girls do you know with a carousel in their front yard?"

"I want to go outside," she said, "to the lady's house."

"That skeleton of a burnt house is no place for a girl to play," he said, laying the manual down, "even if the staircase is in perfectly good condition."

She let go of the case as the hinges of its handle sighed. She heard the sound of her mother dropping a handful of necklaces onto the tile floor of the old house. Nicky held on to the strap, cracking it at Shane like a whip, before twirling the case through the air. She heard her mother's wedding ring graze a bottle of her father's after-shave.

"Quit waving that damn thing in my face," Shane shouted.

"What?" she asked. "I couldn't hear you."

"If you want the carousel, put that case down!"

She held on tighter.

That week Shane scattered lemons all over his house. At night, she heard a clink and saw the glasses glinting when the headlights of a passing car shone on her window. She thought of his Adam's apple bobbing on his throat while he drank. She listened for the heavy, sinking sound of his swallow, which reminded her of a man dropping a child into a lake. Her mattress level with the tabletops, she fell asleep breathing lemon air.

Shane's house was full of books she wasn't allowed to open and trinket boxes he hadn't offered to unlatch. He didn't have much furniture, only a piano that didn't play, a few round tables littered with gyroscopes and yo-yos, and a giant ironwood chair stacked with leather cushions.

Shane said the chair was priceless and weighed over two hundred pounds. The legs were carved into lions' paws resting on solid globes. The chair's arms tapered off in two women's round faces. She pinched one of the women's noses. On the crest was a jester crying smooth tears.

She took an empty glass off the piano and pretended to drink. On the walls were photographs of the moon in all phases of its cycle and a single wagon wheel rolling past a tumbleweed. Shane's knife collection was locked in a glass display, but Nicky wasn't interested in his tools. She flipped through a heavy book next to the carpenter's manual and found pictures of jigsaws and diagrams of windmills and carousels. Her name was written in pencil under the drawing of a lighthouse. She tried to rub it out with her finger.

She felt it was her duty to tamper with possessions that were not her own. The many questions she had wanted to ask her mother should have been spread out across her entire lifetime. Even if she had known her parents' end was near, there would have been no time to ask such questions before the storm.

She put the book down and reached for a pearly trinket box. Opening the latch, she found a steel marble, fish bones, and a wooden doll on a chain. She untangled the doll, gave her case a single pat, and dropped the chain into her pocket. It poured in like a narrow stream of water.

Shane walked into the room and the trinket box fell to the floor. "What are you doing?" he asked, looking at his throne.

"I dropped it."

The fish bones rattled awhile after fracturing into scattered shards.

"Where's the doll? I made it as a surprise for you. But you can't keep out of my things, and now you've ruined it," he said, his eyeballs rolling behind his round glasses.

She motioned to the floor by tapping her shoes.

"Bring it here, or you don't get your carousel," he said.

"You're not my mom." Holding the case close to her ear like a giant seashell, she heard the river rolling over a tree that had fallen into its water.

"Do it."

"You're not my dad." She clutched the case tighter and listened for the metallic moan of the garage door opening at her parents' house. Instead, she heard the key turning in the doorknob of the burned house on the hill.

"You think you're so smart with your little case, don't you?"

As she swung around to walk away, she heard her mother's wedding ring hit the handle of the teacup.

The tip of Shane's pencil scratched furiously in the margins of the carpenter's manual. The sound was more terrible than the talons of a hawk on a string clutching a banister. Nicky lay her head on the case and heard her father talking to the fierce birds he used for hunting, the silence of the dust from the owls' wings falling as the barn doors opened.

She held the case over her belly as she crept near Shane to see what he was writing. He was sitting in his enormous chair.

"What now?" he asked. The pencil stopped moving. She had seen two words written in scrawling letters – *over roof* – before Shane closed the manual gently on his long finger.

Place markers with frayed edges stuck out from between the pages, causing the manual to bulge thickly in Shane's hands. The cover was slick and barely blue where the letters of the title had been rubbed away. A photograph fell out of the manual.

Nicky stepped back. Shane opened the manual slowly while keeping his gaze fixed on her. She looked down at the case in her hands and smiled.

"Do you want me to take that away from you?" he asked, reaching for the photograph. "You're tempting me, right? You're so cute with that little key dangling from your necklace."

"Am not." When she tossed the case into the air and caught it, she heard her father's razor snagging on her mother's lace garter, the hands of the old clock clanging against a tiny green light bulb inside.

"What's in there anyway?"

"Plenty."

Shane kept his right hand inside the manual. With his left arm, he reached down slyly. Nicky saw him reclaim the black-and-white photograph of a woman leaning over a chair. He put it back inside the manual, unaware that another had slipped out.

Nicky laughed to herself. The other photograph had fallen under the shadow of the piano bench. She tried to look away from where it had landed. Shane watched her with squinting eyes as he straightened in his chair.

"What's so funny?" he asked, the sweat trickling from under the curls of his dark hair onto his forehead.

"Can't say." She was amused by the trembling in his voice. She balanced the case high on her head and curtsied slowly.

"Oh, I think you can."

She started to shiver. The case fell to the floor and rolled away from her toward Shane. She heard a single jingle bell tumbling into a porcelain pepper shaker inside. Shane stopped the case with the shiny, pointed toes of his shoes.

"What did you see?" he asked. "Nicky, who was in the photograph?"

"I didn't see."

He kicked the case across the floor to her. She leaned over it as it slowed down. The glass cover of a small frame cracked against the lip of a wine bottle. The cork was also inside. When the case hit the wall, she heard her mother's violin falling to the floor, the delicate neck breaking in three exquisite places, the strings crossed and bent.

Nicky crawled under the piano bench, holding the case between her ankles to keep her arms and hands free. When she picked up the photograph, she let out a long breath of air, whistling through her bottom teeth. It was black-and-white, a picture of a boy about her age fishing in a river valley. She thought the boy had Shane's cutting eyes. The boy's river could have been the one she left behind, but in the photograph the trees looked shorter along the bank and the rocks more jagged.

She scraped the boy's face off the slick paper with her fingernails. She ran into the dark closet in the room where she slept and slipped the river photograph into her case.

When she shook the case, she jostled the bottle of her father's after-shave and heard the sound of his skipping a flat rock over the water. In her parents' house, no matter where she stood, she had been able to hear the river rushing over the hills not far away. Her dark horse, Canbury Green, often leaned over in silence to drink from its edge.

She had seven strands of her horse's mane and shavings from its hooves inside her case. But she would not touch them. She listened for the hoof shavings twanging darkly against a twig from the silver maple that once rustled outside her bedroom window.

It had been her sleeping tree. The thin branches twitched at the slightest movement of an owl landing. The white-gray bottoms of the blown leaves were the last interesting colors she had seen every night before she closed her eyes under the shadow-canopy of her old room. But the night of the storm she watched the leaves thrashing as branches were torn away by the wind, shattering her window. The damaged tree was not what she chose to remember. She remembered the house the way it was, the window before it was broken, and the maple tree while it was still whole.

Thoughts of silver leaves still made her yawn. She had three of them tucked away inside her case. When she scuffed it against the closet walls, she heard the leaves crackling and the static sounds of her mother's long robe picking up electricity on the carpet, her mother's frightened cry when her charged fingertips touched the doorknob.

Nicky didn't have the tree to herself for long. She had been waiting at her window the morning after the Scygazers' party, looking out past the damaged trunk, waiting for her father's car to pull into the driveway. She heard the rumbling of Shane's black truck instead. The silver maple was dying. Too many of its branches had broken off during the storm.

When Shane told her to pack her things, he was holding an ax to the maple trunk. She ran inside, flung the case out of the wastebasket, then ran with it all over the house and the land. She pulled tassels off curtains, wicks out of candles, pages out of encyclopedias. Anything she admired she broke into small pieces. She took the best of the pieces with her. She gathered her father's clippers, laces from his boots, strands of his beard. She kept her mother's lip-gloss, the glass lids of her mother's perfume bottles. She chose smooth, amber stones from the river, cattails, a tiny bottle filled with its water.

After collecting, she went back inside her parents' house where Shane had been pacing, his breath ragged and strange.

"Was it you?" he asked. "Oh my God, was it you who tore this place apart?"

Before they left, he picked up her mother's violin and threw it across the kitchen tile. Nicky reached for a few of its splinters.

Now there were only two rules for collecting: first, every item had to be small enough to fit inside the case; second, she had to take what she wanted without being seen. Most of the time, the items were of little value to others: a dog's tooth, a feather off a dead bird, a sliver of Shane's toenail. But if she needed something that already belonged to someone else, the owner was no matter as long as she kept to the rules.

So far, she had taken a barrette out of a little girl's hair, a pair of scissors from an old woman's pocket, the handle off a toilet, the tag off a cat's collar. She especially didn't want Shane to discover the pouch of lemon seeds she had gathered from his water glasses. Next summer she hoped to be far away from the carousel, planting a grove of citrus trees by the river.

At the moment, she had her eyes on the one item that would be harder to collect than all the others. Although Shane rarely laughed, he had a nice, bright smile because of the tiny, white diamond glinting in between his front teeth. Once she had slipped the diamond into her case and heard it rolling into the keyhole, she would drop the key inside, leaving the latch clamped shut forever.

*   *   *

After straightening the frames on the walls, Shane paced by the windows with a satisfied expression. He made more frantic notes in his manual, stopping occasionally to sharpen his pencil with a knife he took out of his pocket. Sometimes he would whittle the pencil down to nothing, then begin a long spell of cursing, as if he just realized what he had done. When he left to search for another pencil, Nicky crept toward the manual. But he was never gone long enough for her to lay her hands on it.

She heard the sputtering of a truck engine shutting off. She ran with the case to the window. She saw Shane signing a piece of paper and three men in yellow shirts unloading wooden boxes from their truck. They carried six trunks into Shane's living room, then left without a word. Shane came in with a crow bar. As he began hacking and prying at the lids, Nicky waited for him to unpack intricate painted horses. Instead, he uncovered her mother's dresses drowning in Styrofoam chips.

He threw the dresses aside as carelessly as if he were handling old newspapers. Some of the silk snagged and ripped on the trunk's edge.

"Come on. Come on," he said. "Where is it?"

He tossed away her mother's lace robes and her father's shoes. Bottles of her mother's makeup shattered on the floor. He flung a portrait of her parents in its glass frame at the window. He slowly lifted the lid of the cigar boxes that contained her father's coin collection, then let the coins fall gently through his fingers.

Nicky lay down on the dresses and took in the scent of her mother's sachet balls. She began tearing the buttons off the dresses. They were made of cut glass and shell. When the case bounced lightly on her hip, the buttons sounded like hail hitting her mother's open parasol.

The evening light was still warm. The shadow of herself and her case stretched out long and narrow on the road before her. She heard the hard bottoms of her shoes tapping the asphalt softer than the hooves of Canbury Green. Inside her case, the tip of a dart pecked at a yellow pool ball. She heard the pregnant lady talking to her parakeet before the rain came.

A few of the neighborhood dogs had gathered at the burned house. Two red Chows and a German shepherd were fighting over a can leaking yellow liquid. Nicky raked her fingers through the white-gray powder covering the rubble. The ashes were the color of the silver maple but as dull and scattered as the life that remained after the thunder. She found the door of a birdcage, the shell of a small turtle, a paintbrush, a metal ruler, a pacifier on a string. She picked up a jointed bone so tiny it might have been a sparrow toe.

She climbed to the top of the staircase to watch the dog fight die down below her. She saw Shane running up the road, his hair blowing as his head turned abruptly from side to side. He was calling her name.

He came to the edge of the concrete foundation but didn't step onto its surface. "Nicky," he said, looking around at the other houses, "what are you doing up there? Come down."

"Never." She sat down on her case. The buttons spilled over the hoof shavings inside. She heard Canbury Green galloping out of the barn before the summer storm.

"You have to come down sometime, don't you? When you do, I'll be home waiting."

"Come up here and get me. What are you afraid of?"

"I don't have time to play games."

She watched him walk back to his house and shut the door. The wind died down first to a breeze then to silence. The dogs looked at her for an instant and went on fighting.

She walked slowly back to Shane's house. The light was fading fast, and there was no place left for her to go. She expected him to be waiting. But the house was quiet inside. In the living room, the shadow of the throne stretched across the floor. She felt afraid until she saw the carpenter's manual sitting by itself in the center of a small, round table.

She picked up the manual and ran with it into the bathroom. She set the manual and her case down beside the tub and turned on the water. She shed her clothes, dropping her shirt on top of the case. She heard the river rushing and her mother dropping bath beads into the water.

She stepped into the tub, reached over its side, picked up the manual by its spine. It was heavy in her hands. She was careful not to drop it as she spread it open on her knees and began to flip through its pages. The inside cover read, "To Shane from Grandpa Newly." She couldn't remember much about Grandpa

Newly, who had died years ago, only the clicking noises he had made with his dentures to make her smile.

An envelope slipped out from the pages. She opened it and found photographs of a woman polishing a table, painting a picture of a forest, holding a small bird on her finger.

The steam from the bath water was beginning to crinkle the pages. Nicky studied the sketches of watch gears, guitar saddles, oval-backed chairs. Articles had been clipped and pasted onto the pages. She read their titles: THE CAROUSEL, A THING OF BEAUTY, ON CARVING HORSES, MECHANICS AND MOTION. Her name was written under a drawing of the giant water wheel of a steamboat.

She heard footsteps in the hall and dropped the manual into the water. When she tried to squeeze the pages dry, they stuck together. The manual had swollen to twice its size. She heard Shane's breathing outside the door and dressed in a hurry. She stuck her head through an armhole of her shirt and slipped on the slick floor in terror.

The manual was still dripping when she handed it to Shane. The dark ink stained her wrists and palms. She leaned against the case, securing it against her back and the wall. As she shifted, she felt the case slipping and heard the heel of her mother's shoe touch down on the staircase.

When Shane took the manual from her, he held it in silence as if he didn't know what it was. She felt afraid for her case. She began to walk away with it.

"This has been in the family for generations," Shane said, smoothing his hands over the wet cover. "I kept a record of everything, everything." He began to wipe the cover on his pant legs. "How the hell am I supposed to build the carousel without it?"

Shane was smiling the day the carousel kit came in a silver truck. He arranged the cut wood in an arc on his gravel yard. He slit the cardboard boxes with his pocketknife. Inside were more boxes full of sawdust, planks tied with cord, and discs of all sizes.

"Don't say I never did anything for you, honey. You and that little black case."

"You mind your own business. You're not my daddy," she said. She put her ear to the case and heard her father in his heavy boots stepping into the river.

Shane swallowed hard. "Thank God for that."

She loved the smell of the new wood, like a whole forest had been cut down to nothing. While Shane hammered, she tapped on the sides of her case. The way the carousel was turning out, all splintery and lop-sided, made her want to run to the house lightning had struck. Inside her case, a teaspoon hit the lens of a camera, making a sound like a single drop of rain hitting the tin roof of the barn.

"You stay here, now," Shane said. He dropped the hammer and ran his fingers through his hair. A glossy strand fell away. She walked over the round base. "You're a good girl," he said. When he turned away from her and started hammering again, she picked up the single hair. He turned back to her suspiciously. "I'm not doing all this work for nothing, am I?"

"No," she said. The staircase loomed, twisted, on the hill, as charred and spare as a backbone after the flesh had been burned away.

"So you like your carousel?"

He was out in the yard hammering every day that week. She had nothing to do but watch every thundering moment surrounded by unfinished wood and horses impaled on long poles. They were leaning on each other and badly formed. They seemed to her not really horses at all. She threw the case into the air and caught it again and again. From the inside came the sound of hooves coming down on the meadowland.

"Nothing will ever take the place of my Canbury Green," Nicky said.

Shane spilled a bucket of nails on the circle base. "I should have known better than to start this," he said, picking up a hammer. He had already secured the umbrella canopy. "You were spoiled rotten by the time you came to me, and now nothing I could do would ever please you." He looked down at the new scuffmarks on his shoes. "Your daddy should have never given you a real horse to ride."

"Canbury Green," she said, swinging the case over her hair.

"Why don't you name one of the carousel horses?"

"I want to go to the lady's house," Nicky said. She dropped the case to the ground and heard the pacifier hit the metal ruler.

"What lady?"

"The pregnant lady on the hill who left when the storm came."

"What do you want with her?"

"I'll give one of the horses her name."

"Like hell you will. I never knew it anyway."

"So," Nicky said, rocking the case in her arms. She heard the sparrow bone hit her mother's curler.

"Maybe she wasn't even pregnant. She might have been just fat. A rich woman, young and living alone, she had the finest house on the block."

"And it burnt down," Nicky said. Inside her case, the paintbrush fell on her father's clippers. She thought she heard the camel-hair bristles swipe over the velvet.

"I only saw her from far away," he said, "high up on her little hill. Serves her right, trying to live above the rest of us."

Nicky put her face on the case and began to shiver.

"That's not what I meant," Shane said, dropping the hammer. "God, that sounded awful. I've been working like a dog these last couple of days. I never really knew her. I shouldn't have brought you to her house."

"I was sorry that night when I saw the fire," he said, sitting down on the carousel. "It had been storming a long time. I thought I heard a baby cry a little before the thunder."

*　　　*　　　*

Shane painted the carousel blue, white, and gold. Nicky noticed the horses had no distinguishable manes or tails. He waited for the paint to dry before he put on another coat. Gold enamel flaked over the horses' eyes.

"Get on," he said, but there were no painted saddles and no music. The carousel wasn't turning. He helped her onto the back of what she thought was a blue dog. From where she sat, the neighborhood was carved up into long sections by the gold poles. In the middle of the carousel was a large, white box with a door. Shane walked into it as if it were a closet.

"It's powered by wind," he said, coming out. "But I have to start the gears turning."

He grabbed on to one of the poles and started running. The carousel picked up speed until the house was a blur. She held on tighter to the black case. The staircase on the hill was just a white streak. She heard the scissors hit the dog's tooth and shouted, "Slow down." Dobermans, not horses, were rushing in on every side.

"I don't know how," Shane was saying as he ran with the pole still in his hands.

The neighborhood eventually stopped turning. The bottle of river water cracked against the bottle of her father's after-shave. As Shane lifted her off the blue dog, splinters cut into her legs.

"What's the matter?" he asked while she was still in his arms. "Don't you like your carousel? That was only the first pony," he said. "You've still got twelve more left to ride."

"I hurt my leg," she said, holding on to her case with both hands. Water began to trickle out of a crease on the lid. As the glass bead skipped over the shards of the broken bottles, she heard her mother singing in the shower.

"Want me to kiss it and make it better?"

She saw the white diamond flare twice before he puckered his lips. Through the dark hole in his mouth, it glinted in her direction like a baby bird's winking eye.

He was laughing hard and trying to cover up the diamond while he smiled. "Did you really think I was going to kiss you?" he asked.

She spat in his eye. Shane dropped her on the gravel. She got up and kicked the horse she had been riding. When its slender leg broke apart, she saw it was as delicate and hollow as her mother's violin.

She tried to run away, but Shane was right behind her. She felt his hand touching her arm. As she ran faster, the case bounced hard on her right knee. Inside, the lemon seeds poured out of the pouch and trickled over her mother's wedding ring, the dog's tooth, the blue bottle, and one of Shane's eyelashes. When she lifted the case over her head to put the strap around her neck, she heard the woman who used to live in the burned house pouring cereal into a bowl before the storm.

Nicky climbed to the top of the stairs and lay down on the case. She could see the carousel below her turning by itself on the wind. Shane hesitated a moment before stepping onto the house's foundation. He towered above her, sobbing until his whole body shook the stairs. When he finally smiled again, Nicky thought she saw the diamond slipping out of his front teeth or a fleck of spittle catching the sunlight as it fell. She almost reached for it.

With one hand, his fingers clutching her hair, Shane lifted her body off the highest stair. The latch on her case broke apart. Her collection fell through the air: her mother's wedding ring, the teacup handle, the glass bead, the white top of the flower, gone. A strand of Shane's hair and a bird's feather blew far past the dog's tooth.

"You're not my mommy. You're not my daddy," she kept saying, the lid of the empty case flapping like the wing of a stunned bird.

He carried her down the stairs. From far away, the carousel looked beautiful, horses, not Dobermans, leaping in a swirl of blue and gold.

SYMPATHY IN THE RED ROOM

Eva settled into a barstool and watched Sammie pour a caipirinha into a chilled, old-fashioned glass filled with crushed ice. The jigger, the strainer, the bar spoon, the shaker, the citrus reamer, and the muddler were parts of speech in the cocktail of coded language they shared together.

Tonight Eva wanted to test Sammie's memory.

"Do you remember me?"

"There's nothing worse than a foamy Bloody Mary. You have to go easy. It's a drink that has to be rolled from one glass to another, never shaken."

After mixing a large Bloody Mary, Sammie refilled a pitcher of light beer. The jukebox was blaring Hendrix's "The Wind Cries Mary." Eva realized the song's timing was an odd coincidence and wondered whom the drink was for. Two old men were playing darts in the far corner, smoking cigars. Sammie took a sip of the Bloody Mary herself, raising the glass to her mouth as she looked toward Eva.

Stilettos echoed on the pavement outside the open door as women leaped over gutters near The Recluse. Three false entrances were in plain sight. The real entrance was disguised from street view. Eva didn't know why she kept coming back.

The windows were boarded with wood planks, and she was afraid of Sammie.

Eva made small talk about the drinks as Sammie mixed them. By speaking only of bartending and the local gossip traded by the regulars, Eva learned much about cocktails and almost nothing about Sammie's new life with the woman who owned the bar and lived in the apartments upstairs.

Lately, the owner had stopped coming out of her apartment. Even though the changes in the bar were odd, Eva couldn't help watching Sammie carry food trays up the private stairway at the back of the building. Sammie had taken over the business of managing the bar so that the owner never had to leave her rooms.

The owner was nowhere to be seen. Eva believed she was hiding, perhaps in a place where she could watch her customers without them watching her.

On the other side of the bar, a large man in a dark blue suit was sitting alone at a table near the window, looking out at the rain. He was handsome in a sad way. His face was unshaven, and he seemed so lonely that Eva wanted to sit beside him and hold his hand, just to talk about the rain.

"That's Silas Scott, the psychologist," Sammie said.

"Never heard of him."

Sammie muddled the superfine sugar with the bitters, the orange slice, the cherry, and the soda with a generous amount of bourbon.

"You know the owner, right? She claims he's the wrong type. I'll be glad when he's gone. So will she."

"Why?"

"She called the police, but they couldn't do nothing. He had photographs of her. This is the weird thing – she could never figure out who the photographer was or even when the photographs were taken. She couldn't even recognize the rooms in some of the photographs."

After wiping her hands with a rag and garnishing the glass with an orange slice and a cherry, Sammie walked to Silas's table and set the Old Fashioned down. She walked away in a hurry, without speaking.

When Sammie returned to her, Eva was pleased but struck by an awkward silence. This had been the most illuminating conversation she'd had with Sammie since the night they compared the shapes and colors of various tequila bottles lined up on the display shelf in front of the mirror. The cost of vodka was another engrossing topic, how to determine the best brands and the standards for their purity. Grey Goose was Sammie's choice. Eva favored Pearl, which *Playboy* magazine had hailed as one of the best new vodkas of the year. Even though she preferred red wine to vodka, she knew which vodka fit her lifestyle – winter wheat and mountain water distilled five times, yet cheap enough to fit a schoolteacher's budget.

After drinking four glasses of the house red, Eva ordered another, against her better judgment.

"This one's on you," she called out to Silas Scott, and began walking toward the window where he sat. Sammie mouthed "No." Eva ignored her. Silas didn't turn around to her.

His confused expression in the glass seemed to change only slightly as her reflection moved toward his.

"I'm not a smoker," she said to him, sitting down in the empty chair at his table.

"You look like a smoker," Silas said, his voice soft yet gruff, husky as if his throat were damaged from years of cigarettes.

"Must be the dark circles under my bloodshot eyes."

"Maybe."

"You're a very sad man." Standing up, Eva fell out of her chair. She had wanted to go back to Sammie, but she was suddenly confused, disoriented, and emotional from the wine. Silas caught her arm. She steadied herself by placing her hands on the floor, her face bent down to her knees.

"You have a nice ass, honey, but you're drunk," he said, helping her back into the chair, "and I'm not paying for your drink."

He slipped a cigarette into his mouth and lit it quickly just as she opened her lips to reply. She had wanted to talk just to keep him from talking. For some reason, all the terrible things he was saying about her made him seem more attractive. He looked her directly in the eye as if her drunkenness and her rudeness didn't put him off.

"So you're an ass man, not a breast man or a leg man?"

"I'm just a man."

"I heard something weird happened with the owner, something really fucked up, Silas. Did she have a nice ass?"

"A lot of fucked-up things happen."

"But I want to hear your side of the story."

"No."

"I'm just the opposite of a repressed person. I'm not that good at remembering names and places and numbers and things like that. But as far as actual experiences, I feel like I remember almost everything that ever happened to me, even the little things. Test me. Ask me anything about any time in my life."

"You could be repressing something right now, and you would never know it."

"But I just know that I'm not."

"You're not listening. That's what repression is. People who are really repressing something have no idea they're repressing it. They feel just like you, like nothing's wrong, like they remember everything."

He signaled to Sammie, pointing to Eva, and Sammie brought another Old Fashioned and another glass of wine to the table, taking away the empty glasses.

As Eva drank her wine, she ordered another.

"It's too much," he said as Sammie held the glass out to her.

Eva tried to stand again. Silas stood up, reaching out to help her. She tripped and spilled the full glass of wine on his boots. Without thinking, she let go of the glass and stood motionless to watch it fall. The wineglass shattered near her feet, splattering her stilettos.

She felt her bra straps slip down her shoulders so that she had to adjust herself in front of him. Her face burning, she reminded herself she had inherited her large breasts from her mother's side of the family. Even though she knew it was warped logic, she blamed her mother whenever her breasts got in the way – every time her nipple accidentally brushed against a stranger's elbow in a crowded room, every time she felt a man's eyes cautiously wandering away from her face to her chest.

Silas was a big man with a thick torso. She hadn't realized how tall he was until he stood next to her. Tall men made her nervous. He smelled faintly of sweat and sawdust and beer and the cigarettes he had been smoking. She only glanced at his eyes before looking away.

Sammie found a thin rag on the edge of the bar and bent down to pick up the shattered glass.

"Careful," he whispered to Sammie. "Don't cut yourself. It's my fault. Let me do it."

"No," Eva said. "Let me."

"I don't know if that's such a good idea."

Sammie walked away, cradling the larger pieces of glass in a bundle of paper towels.

Silas leaned against the railing near the doorway. Eva crouched down to wipe the wine off him. Even though she knew he was looking down her shirt while she leaned over his feet, she didn't put her hand over her chest.

As she dried his boots, the wet cloth deteriorated on the black leather, ripping apart under her fingers. In that helpless position, she felt her vagina opening, the way her feet were splayed under her legs, the weight of her hips resting on her heels, her narrow ankles buckling as she crouched over his boot tips.

210

"Why are you shaking?" he asked.

"I'm not." She tried to look up at him, blinking hard.

"You are. Look at your hands. They're practically all over the place."

"They're fine."

"Hey? Why won't you look at me? You know it's rude not to look at a man when he's talking to you?"

What kind of psychologist wears silver-tipped cowboy boots, she asked herself, and suddenly felt more comfortable. She handed him the rag.

"I got most of the wine off. Your boots should be fine. If not, I'll buy you another pair."

"That won't be necessary." He reached out a hand to help her off her feet.

Like the horses in the fields outside her window, Eva was wary of strangers, easily spooked, even by her own shadow scaling the walls at night. She felt she had to be afraid of the darkness. While she was sometimes lonely during the days, she was often terrified during the nights that someone would find her and hurt her.

Pain was all about seeing. If no one ever saw her, no one would ever think to hurt her. But if she lived her life unnoticed, she would also live her life alone. That was why painting fascinated her. Artists could create images from their imaginations, painting an image so fully it seemed real, but there was no way for anyone to reach the image, to harm the thing itself because it never really existed outside of the painting and the painter's mind.

Once when she was nineteen, as she unbraided her long hair, she sat across from her mother on her mother's bed. That night, like many nights, she wondered why the man had broken into their house, what he had wanted, and what he had seen in the house that made him target her among all the other people in the town. What drew him to her and her mother? By the time she began to wonder about the real question – what he had done to her mother once he broke inside – Eva was thirty-one, sitting alone on the same bed in her mother's house, and her mother had been dead for seven years.

Most of all, she remembered the window glass shattering onto the carpet, the glittering shards in the lamplight as the lamp turned over, rolling across the living room floor until the cord stretched too far and came unplugged. Her mother's screams trailed into silence. No one came to help. She didn't call the police, but only sat quietly beside the dark lamp, the window glass cutting into the backs of her legs as she held her knees to her chest and went to sleep. As dawn broke, the gray light came through the windows, and she heard her mother talking on the phone. Her mother's unmarried sister, Aunt Mellissa, arrived at the house soon after the call. Mellissa said for Eva not to worry, that everything would be all right if she would just go to her room, close the door, and leave her mother alone for a while.

No one ever spoke of that day, or the night before. And everything was all right, her life going on as it had before the window was broken. Years later, as she talked to her mother in the hospital room, she tried to ask her mother about the man. Her mother was in the last stages of lupus. She thought the disease might inspire some honesty during their long visits.

"Do you remember the man?"

"What man?"

"The one who broke the window that night?"

"What night? A boy from the neighborhood broke the window playing golf on his parents' front lawn. Boy, was he in trouble. His parents made him pay for everything. He had to deliver papers all summer just to cover the damage. It was a nice, expensive window, antique-style beveled glass."

"Mom."

"He did."

In her old high school, Eva often forgot she was a teacher and felt as if she were a student again. Feeling lost and confused, looking for Sammie in the halls, Eva was afraid to look into her students' eyes after looking at their paintings. Sometimes she expected her mother to be waiting for her in the house when she walked back home. In her art class, she encouraged creativity, allowing her students to paint anything they wanted to paint, any image that came to their minds, never asking them to explain what the images meant or where they came from.

When Eva and Sammie were students in the old high school, after painting each other into odd compositions, they couldn't explain what the images meant. Sammie painted Eva with eagle wings soaring among gulls with dead presidents' faces, the shadow of the wings spelling *charlatan* over an ocean of fire. Eva painted Sammie completely nude with a blue saxophone strapped to her back as she walked to a red phone booth at the end of a lonely highway.

Their art teacher had taken them into his office and said, "I don't get it. What's going on here?"

They looked at him for a long time, but didn't say anything. He started laughing.

Afterward, Eva moved her easel to the opposite side of the studio, and Sammie stared at her canvas without painting. Eva avoided Sammie and stopped speaking to her.

Twelve years later, Eva wandered into the bar and struck up a conversation with the owner, a small woman with long dark hair that hid her face as she stood in the shadows. Startled to find Sammie mixing drinks, Eva allowed the owner to introduce Sammie as if they had never known each other at all, and the owner seemed satisfied by their deception.

Eva never understood Sammie's willingness to participate in the lie. The owner's nervous movements, suspicious glances, and strange, hawklike beauty were enough to fuel Eva's desire to deceive her. She seemed to be a woman who did not want to know the truth.

The owner hurriedly counted receipts behind the bar, perhaps willing to believe her employees and her customers were people with no pasts, even though their families had been living together for generations in the same, small, east Texas town.

"God, this is a disappointment," Eva said in the parking lot, her stilettos soaked in a puddle of rain and motor oil. "Why don't you just take a knife and shoot me through the heart?"

"A gun, you mean?"

"Whatever."

Silas walked to the passenger side of his car, unlocking the door and opening it for her. As he helped her get in, he slid his hand under her legs. She was too drunk to do anything about it, so she waited until he was under her, gripping her cheeks, and sat down on his hand.

"Is there any way I can have my hand back? I need it to drive."

She shifted her weight slightly so he could free himself from her.

As he drove through the dark streets, she gave him directions to her house, all along realizing something was wrong.

"You might want to turn on your headlights so you can see the road."

"What if I don't want to see the road?"

"Suit yourself."

He helped her out of the car and approached her house by the side door, as if he lived there. Reaching into her purse, he took out her car keys and unlocked the door for her.

"Come on in and make yourself comfortable," he said.

After following him inside to the living room, she stood in front of the fireplace.

"Go ahead and make a fire," she said. "The wood's good and dry, and the matches are on the mantel. There's old newspapers in the metal bin."

"All right."

"My horses are out there." She pointed to the window that looked out onto the field. "But it's kind of hard to see dark horses in the night."

He struck a match against the brick. The match broke. She wanted to see if he was capable of starting the fire on his own.

In the powder bathroom, she carefully prepared herself for him. After removing all her clothes with the lamplight warm against the red walls, she turned in circles in front of the long mirror on the bathroom door. She bent over to admire her hips, to see what she looked like from behind. Sometimes when she forgot about the scar, she thought her rump was her finest feature, soft yet firm, and she thought it was a pity so few people had seen it this way.

Standing near the marble sink, she ran water over a white cloth to wash her vagina, gently opening the lips after sitting on the tile to examine herself with a little mirror, just to contemplate the pinkness inside her that she rarely saw. Wanting to look nice for Silas, she considered the shape of her pubic hair. She could shave it off so that it looked like a little girl's or she could shape it into a slim line or even a mohawk. Instead, she decided to leave it in the familiar V shape that pleased her most.

When she came out of the bathroom in her red high heels and translucent robe, Silas was nowhere to be found. His car was no longer in the driveway. So, after looking for him in the other rooms, she poured a glass of cheap wine and fell asleep in front of the fire. Sleeping fitfully, she woke several times, terrified by an odd sensation that there was someone else in the house, walking through the rooms above her. Every time she worked up the courage to investigate, she felt too tired to stand.

When she woke Saturday morning, with a familiar dry mouth and headache, she searched her house, room by room, and thought her mother's old room seemed different. The perfume bottles were out of order, the photographs that usually hung on the walls had been taken down and laid out on the bed, the window was open, and the record player was on. Although the jazz record was turning, the needle was resting on the hook, and the volume was turned down to the lowest notch.

Since her childhood, Eva had adorned her body in distinct ways, using odd methods of her own design. Disguising the curved scar on her hip, she accentuated other areas of her body, calling attention to the length and delicate shape of her neck and waist with crimson and gold chokers, coral necklaces, and woven belts made of cranberry leather. Red jewelry collected from antique shops had been her passion until she discovered she could make a paste of honey and water to glue petals to her skin.

Shortly after her mother's death, she had an affair with a body painter. Trading sex for transient art, she lay down on a wooden floor covered in white cloth. He stenciled her belly in overlays of blue-toned red, making long veins that led down her legs and back up to her breasts. Just before he finished, he etched black and gray shadows with a small airbrush over the stenciled leaves, adding orange-red splotches and gold tones where the light hit. For months after he left her, she was convinced that he had stained her somehow, and she was satisfied with her body until the stain began to fade away, leaving her skin clear again so that the scar stood out. She had no idea where the scar came from, so she didn't like to answer lovers who asked her why the scar was there.

Now, she thought after dismantling the hibiscus flowers and gluing the petals down in large patches like a second skin over her body, at least she would smell like honey and her skin would look more attractive. Out of habit, she dressed in black slacks and a black sweater, making sure the pasted petals were disguised under her clothes.

In the fireplace, local newspapers from her hometown, the headlines dated back twenty years ago, burned to black ash, rustling like dark feathers under the flames. Eva stood in front of the green-glass mirror, smoking a cigarette, whispering to herself in a dusky voice that reminded her of her mother. Her lovely Aunt Mellissa was in the black-and-white photographs, looking as young as Eva's mother and standing next to the man who had gone missing. He was never found. Even though Eva had been burning photographs of him for hours, the day was not yet wasted. Black horses trotted through the fields outside her window, flicking their sleek tails in the rising winds before the dust storm settled over the grasses.

The lace curtains filtered the pale light of evening, soft enough to make her face look like a young girl's in profile. When the shadows fell right, after gently touching the white powder under her eyes, she stuffed hibiscus petals into her bra, dismantling the flowers in the royal-blue vase slowly as if peeling ripe fruit.

Sammie called Eva just as the sky began to darken that evening, but their conversation was interrupted by a loud knock on Eva's front door.

"I have to go," Eva said to Sammie.

Through the window, Eva saw Silas and realized that he was determined to see her. She opened the door. The pale-blue sky had given way to an indigo so true it blotted out the leaves of the neighboring oak trees.

He smiled when she didn't say anything. She didn't smile back. He coughed nervously into his large hand before flicking his gold lighter. The spark flared. The little flame began to shudder like her fingers. She scratched the back of her neck.

Holding the cigarette expertly in his full lips, his mouth worked under the shadow of his beard. Moving his lips to the side, he blew the smoke away from her face. Standing casually on the porch, he leaned against the brick wall. A bottle of red wine in a brown paper bag was tucked under his arm.

"Would you have some wine with me?" he asked, taking a deep drag from his cigarette.

"Yes."

God, she thought, *he's going to touch me. His hands will be all over me. The petals will fall from my breasts to the floor, fall from my body to his feet before I fall, and then I will be afraid to stand up, even though his hands have been all over me. But no, he hasn't touched me yet, hasn't even spoken my name.*

"I mean no," she whispered.

He held the wine bottle out to her. "Which is it? Yes or no?"

"You went through my rooms last night. You were in the house when I was asleep. You looked at things when I didn't know what you were doing."

She switched on the outside lights, on the back of the house, over the garden, so that in the formal living room they could see the floodlights on the leaves outside the picture windows. Large white moths beat against the long glass panes. Their wings left traces of gray powder like the nervous brush of her hands across her face. Her fingers tapped her mouth and chin. The lipstick stained her. When she saw the burgundy streaked across her palm, she worried that she had smeared her face into a harlequin's mask.

Using his eyes as a mirror, she gauged her appearance. He cast pensive glances at her. Through his heavy beard, his tongue swiped across his lips before he smiled. He crumpled the paper bag into a ball and tossed it into the fire. Setting the bottle on the edge of the table, he pulled a silver corkscrew from his jacket pocket.

"You have a very nice house," he said. "I didn't get a chance to tell you last night. I got nervous and left without saying good-bye. Then I came back and found the door unlocked and wanted to see you. You were so drunk, I couldn't wake you. I found you passed out in front of the fire. I'm sorry. I shouldn't have done what I did."

"Why did you go through the rooms?"

"I wanted to find out more about you."

"Did you?"

"I'm not sure. But I like the pictures of you and your mother. She is a very beautiful lady."

"Was."

"You take after her."

The dark green glass against the white of his knuckles startled her. For a moment, she saw her mother's hands, not his. Around midnight, she often drove her mother across the lake roads so her mother could see the dock lights reflected on the dark water. Wasted away to almost half her normal body weight, her mother had grown so slight that in her last days Eva could carry her from one room to another and from the house to the car at night. The frail body in the back of the black car as Eva drove away had seemed like a prepubescent child in the rearview mirror. Those same lights shone on her open eyes, so blue Eva could hardly bear to close them. But she did close them, her hand shaking as the slender shadow of her fingers trembled across the white forehead.

Sex, she thought, would make the sadness go away.

Silas began to pour the wine into two antique high-stemmed glasses rimmed with gold. Striking a long match, she lit the tapered candles, molded rose and violet wax. In the mirror above the mantel, she saw her lip liner was still remarkably intact. In the windowsills, leaves glimmered. Concentrating on the new flames as they lengthened while exposing the wicks, she felt his hand on her shoulder. He held a wineglass to her mouth. The wine sloshed near the edge.

"Why don't we just take our clothes off?" he asked, looking out the windows where the leaves rustled in the wind.

She drank the wine in her glass as fast as she could before reaching for the bottle to pour herself another, knowing how badly she would need it. She gestured to him with a dismissive swipe of her hand, realizing how lonely the night would be.

She would have been the first to admit that she didn't know what she was doing, but he hadn't asked her what she knew, so she acted as if this behavior were perfectly normal to her. Communication was easier this way – no words, just her eyes staring at his body. He looked back at her as he undressed, expecting her to follow.

After his shoes were laid out neatly on the woven rug, he folded his slacks and shorts on the sofa and draped his shirt and jacket over the high-backed chair. Still fully dressed, she sat on the hearth, waiting for him to come to her. Watching him from across the room, she admired his patience. He was a careful man, thorough and graceful in his movements. She liked the belly on him and thought it would be nice to rub against it. Even though she was relatively certain she wanted to make love to him, she also wanted to run out of the house before it was too late to change her mind. After crossing and uncrossing her legs, she needed a closer inspection. She had to examine his body in the firelight before she was certain.

"Are you sure about this?" he asked, walking toward her with his head tilted to match her sideways gaze, his arms hanging loosely at his sides. He shrugged his shoulders when she didn't answer.

Keeping her eyes on his face, she rested her hand on his. Leaning down, he moved his face closer to hers, his eyes just above her eyes so their lashes were almost touching. She leaned in closer to his mouth. "My mother murdered a man once," she whispered over his parted lips, "in this house."

"If you're joking, it's not funny. Don't talk right now. I'd just like to enjoy your body. Your breasts are wonderful."

"There was blood everywhere, in the bathroom."

"God, your ass."

The man's hands were pale and bluish, still and cold, rigid in their grasping as if reaching out to her. Her mother lit the fire in the fireplace with dry wood and stoked the flames day and night so that it burned for weeks at a time. There was a loud, metallic sound of the hammer hitting the concrete porch in the backyard near the garden. After wrapping rubber bands around brown paper bags, their contents rattling like stones, her aunt took the bags outside and smashed them with the hammer like she did in the winters to break the shells off pecans for Christmas cakes.

As Silas kissed her mouth, Eva wondered why she had been able to tell him the very thing she never had the courage to mention to anyone. After the body was disposed of and the house was in order, she knew not to speak about the man to her mother or her aunt, both of whom were well aware of what had happened upstairs when she was a young girl.

Red was her favorite color after that night. Ever since that summer when she turned eleven years old, she wore red stones in her pierced ears. She begged her mother to let her paint her bedroom and bathroom red, the walls as well as the ceiling, a bright crimson that wouldn't fade away. Some people dreamed in black and white, and some dreamed in color, or so she had been told. But she dreamed in red and white, with various shades of pink and lavender. The red walls were always there as a reminder that she couldn't remember what had happened in that room. When she began to menstruate later that year, her mother was relieved. The night Eva saw startling dots of blood on her legs, she felt a cleansing inside.

Her red was a fire color, trapped inside the flames. It calmed her to look into the heat, the embers burning bright as Silas stood before her, stroking her hair. Red was the color of the bathtub when she came home from school and found her mother and her aunt completely nude, cutting off the man's fingertips with a butcher knife taken from the kitchen. Later, she found one of his fingertips, soft yet wrinkled, drying and curling in on itself on the tile in the corner behind the bathroom door.

"Mom, what's this?"

"What's what? Where did you find that? Throw that away and wash your hands."

Usually, whenever she thought about sex, that man was the only man she saw. The man was lost and no longer visited her in the darkness, although when she woke she could still remember the paper bag wrapped around his head with packing string. Even though she could only remember him as dead, she was becoming more and more certain that she had seen him at least once while he was still alive. The memories felt farther away from her now, less jumbled, calmer, slowly ordering themselves as the red faded away, cooling down like the fire behind her.

In a child's voice that sounded so much like her old voice, she could almost hear herself calling him. She had no idea who her real father was, and no one ever spoke of him, although she had never thought that strange before.

"Mother, do I have a father?" she once asked when she was a child.

"Everyone has a father."

"Where is he?"

"He's in the fields and in the air, on the horses' breath and in the trees, nourishing their roots. But don't ask me where he is now. It's impossible to say. He doesn't move like other men. He's never in one place at one time. There's no telling where he'll be tomorrow, but wherever he is, it won't be with us."

The phone was ringing when she removed her blouse and bra. She decided to let it ring, even though she was worried about Sammie, whose voice had sounded so strange earlier that evening. The petals were stuck to Eva's skin so that Silas had to peel them away from her nipples. He suckled her like a child before sliding her slacks down to her ankles. She took off her stockings and let him run his fingers through her coarse, dark hairs. In shocked silence, she felt him slip his pinkie inside her, then watched as he put his pinkie in his mouth as if to savor the flavor.

He began to peel the petals away from the scar.

"No," she said.

He lifted her in his arms and carried her away from the fire before laying her on the rug.

"Open your legs," he whispered, taking her ankles in his hands.

Suddenly, she felt panicked, shy. He didn't force her. Instead, he began to coax her in a tender voice.

"Please," he whispered, "a little more."

Raising her knees in such an awkward way while he stared down at her, she felt uncomfortable. Slowly, she began to relax. Shifting out of that slightly protected position, she let her legs fall apart so that she was spread wide, his eyes focused on her.

His face moved closer to her until she could feel his breath on her vagina just before he began to explore her with his tongue. Even though she wanted to protect herself by crawling away from him, she couldn't move. Her legs began to shake like the branches of a young oak tree in the wind.

In the middle of the night, she felt him wake in her arms. She pretended to be asleep while he drew away from her, dressed, and walked out the front door. She heard his car start and the crunch of tires rolling over the fallen acorns in the driveway.

After she bathed at dawn, the red room seemed vacuous to her. Without the photographs on the walls, there was nothing to catch her eye but the old bed. The ivory shadowboxes and tiny women her aunt had carved above the mantel were gone. In the living room, Eva looked into the fireplace where the last embers were dying out near the old fragments of bone that had slowly resurfaced from the ashes after the burning. That much of the dead man would always be with her. She supposed there were parts of him scattered throughout the fields, decayed long ago, enriching the earth under the oak trees where the horses roamed.

The room would always be red for him because she couldn't help blaming herself for what her mother and aunt had done. His blood was always on her hands, although she had washed it off long ago.

At The Recluse that day, Eva ordered glass after glass of Sangiovese while Sammie poured pitchers of dark beer for the regulars.

"Sam," Eva whispered into her wineglass.

"So what happened with the psychologist?"

"It's a matter of perception."

Sammie leaped over the bar and grabbed Eva's hand, and they were gone, running behind the buildings, through the brick-walled alleys full of old furniture burned by cigarettes and stained by cats and rain.

Eva followed Sammie up a wooden staircase to what looked like a large apartment full of furnished playrooms for children. There was an old-fashioned lace cradle full of porcelain dolls and a kitchenette with a small, plastic yellow oven and a tiny green sewing machine and a short table near shelves stacked with Playdough. The shelves displayed blue, yellow, and red sculptures of people and animals, snowmen, octopuses, and elephants.

"This is where it happened, where all his patients went to pretend they were children, to remember what they had forgotten. The owner of the bar stayed here for days, and by the time she came out, she said she really thought she was a child. I guess that's why she got so scared – when she saw the photos, when she looked at herself in the mirror."

"Was Silas in the photographs?"

"I know it sounds strange, but every time I go here, I start remembering things I didn't know I could remember."

"What's behind that door?"

"That's what I wanted to show you."

Eva opened the door and saw paintings of herself displayed on the walls. In the paintings, she looked like a young girl, her face reflected in windows of familiar houses as she looked in at other girls she used to know years before. Sometimes her face was unrecognizable, superimposed onto the other girls' faces. Her black wings carried her over the dark hills into the night, wherever she wanted to go. Other paintings showed her carrying straw in her mouth to build her large nest, where other girls were hatching from eggs.

"I haven't seen these for so long," Eva said, "I had forgotten what they were like."

"They're like the dreams I used to have long ago," Sammie whispered, "before I stopped remembering my dreams."

"What dreams?"

"And then the dreams are real, and I remember my life is stranger than my dreams."

"What dreams?"

"I dreamed the owner was floating above me, and then I heard a creaking and found her swinging like a doll on a wire in the dark room."

Through fields, darkness fell. Eva combed the horses' manes, smoothing out the tangles while she felt the horses' hot breath on her face. She led the horses through the dry grasses before riding them to the edge of the property line and back, one at a time, until she was exhausted.

When she walked into her house, she felt as if she couldn't breathe and became light-headed, trying to catch her breath, waiting for the air to fill her lungs. Someone had broken in, window glass shattered on the white carpet as it had been years ago.

The door to the red room was closed as usual. When she opened it, Silas was waiting inside, wearing a gray suit, his jacket strewn across the bed.

The room was changed. The curtains were a deep, rich blue and so were the bed pillows. On the walls, he had hung landscapes of the ocean and sky, the blue of his eyes reflected on the water. The bluebirds and the jays stood out on the canvas, textured with real wings built up in layers under the oils along with sand and crushed leaves.

"I had to see you," he said. "I want to tell you what happened with the owner. It wasn't my fault. I didn't do anything."

"Well, here I am."

"No. I mean I want to show you."

After leading her to the bed, he motioned for her to lie down, then looked at her for a long time, never touching her. He whispered in a voice so soft, so tender, she could barely understand his words.

"I want to be with you all the time."

Even though she knew he was taking photographs of her while she slept, she drifted in and out of consciousness with the camera flash. She forgot about the camera in her dreams where she saw sugar cubes glisten on her father's fingers in the moonlight and watched the horses' tongues swipe over his hands. She could never really see the rest of his face. Darkness disguised him along with the shadows that seemed like bruises. She bent over the post of the barbed-wire fence, and he carved his initials into her hip so that he could always claim her. But the scar changed over the years as her mother sanded it down with rough paper so no one could read the letters.

When she heard the hurried *click-click* of Silas's boots on the hall tiles just before he walked out the back door, she didn't feel as if he were running away. She felt as if he were traveling toward a life she would never know. He moved like a criminal, like every man she had ever loved. No one could understand him or track him down, especially not her.

VAN WINDOWS

The boy was a miracle to me when I found him while passing crowded streets three years ago this winter. Only fifteen, he was two years older than I was when I left my parents for another home, starving. He had soft skin like a girl's, a hairless face, and fiery eyes above deep shadows. His cheekbones protruded as if his skull was beginning to rise through his face. His stomach rumbled. When I bent down to kiss his forehead, I saw lice jumping in his tangled auburn hair. Every night for two weeks, I washed his scalp with medicated green shampoo. His tangles turned to curls, and I picked the dead nits out with a fine-toothed comb before the lice were gone for good.

He had been living on expired vitamin pills thrown out in a drugstore Dumpster. The pills had stained his lips and fingers reddish orange. The first time I drove by his corner, I felt him watching me, begging with only his eyes. As I slowed down, he held out his tiny gray-spotted dog. The dog was shivering and so small I thought it might have been a gutter rat. After parking the van, I stepped out onto the sidewalk and approached the boy. He smelled like his dog, a mixture of cocktails, sea salt, and stagnant water.

I loved him when I laid eyes on him. I didn't have a son or a daughter, and I knew I never would. He stayed on the sidewalk, crouching down, the dog whimpering in his long pale hands. He was slouching back against a brick wall. Hunched over, he looked down at his dog for a long time before he finally raised his head to look up at me.

The dusty denim cap he wore shaded his eyes. His lashes were heavy with rain. A gray trench coat was wrapped around his shoulders. He wore three T-shirts under the trench coat. His boots were too big for his feet, and I could tell he was wearing several pairs of socks to keep them from slipping off his ankles. His jeans were full of holes, and I saw an insect weaving in and out of the holes. The dog was biting its paw as if it had fleas, and the boy's face was covered with dirt and tears. I didn't care how filthy he was. I wanted him to be my son.

I beckoned to him with a flick of my wrist and walked back to my black van. He picked up his little dog and followed me without a word. His hands glowed in the streetlights like a photograph exposed too soon – only blinding light, no color.

For months on end, I mothered him, feeding him all he would eat, driving him from one all-night buffet to another until the fried steaks began to stick to his bones. When he grew stronger than me, I no longer felt responsible for what happened to us in the van or on the grasses or in the stale motel rooms during the long nights.

Leaving San Francisco, wrapped up in a blue sheet in the back of my van, I'm home. The boy drives too fast. Who could blame him? No matter where we go, it's always away. Leaning on my elbows, I look at his scraggly hair, dark and long and tangled, in need of a good washing. *We have no shampoo*, I'm thinking. Then I see his green eyes in the rearview mirror, squinting as he studies me. I cover myself to my chin in the faded blanket that he has netted and unnetted with his nervous fingers during the nights we slept in the grasses on the edge of the highway, watching the red-tailed hawk soar through the morning.

Even after all this traveling, I'm still not certain who he is or where he came from. One night he said his name was Jeremy. The next night it was George. Over the years, I've lost track of some of his names, and I miss the way they felt, whispering as I spoke them, knowing I was giving a voice to his lie. Tonight he's Abe again, maybe because he knows I like that name best. Of all the others, it somehow rings true. Perhaps so I couldn't trace his roots by the sound of his voice, his slow southern accent gradually became Jersey, then British, French, and Italian before he let the Spanish come through on the edge of his whisper. The edge defined itself and deepened in his words until I felt it lingering. Taking hold in a natural progression as he spoke to me, it never went away.

Tonight the van jerks and sputters as it picks up speed so that I have to brace myself against the singed red carpets, my fingernails digging into the synthetic fibers. The boy slams down the brakes, and I fall against the wall, hitting my head on the window.

"Fuck," he says. "Did you feel that? That was a close one. You better be glad I'm driving tonight and not you."

I hold my head in my hands as he pulls over onto the shoulder and drives through the weeds outside of a gated field. The horses walk so slowly I can barely see them for all the darkness. He crawls through our scattered belongings to lie next to me.

Running my hands over his face, I linger near his lips so he can kiss my wrists. His kisses are still a surprise to me, his tenderness like nothing I've experienced before knowing him. His skin is so smooth above the shadow of his new beard, he seems too perfect to be loved by someone like me. I feel his breath on my ear and know I don't deserve to touch him. Maybe no matter how long he stays with me, I will always feel guilty for holding him, even when he's holding me so tight I fear my ribs will crack against his chest.

In Los Angeles, years before I started living in the van, I killed a man. He had been good to me in his own way, I suppose.

The van was red and white then, with silver trim, not black like it is now. I have painted it several times and changed the plates whenever I could. Whenever I have to paint the van, I'm sorry for what I've done. But I know why I did it.

The man was at least twice as heavy as I am. I am a little woman, thin but not as fragile as I appear. He smothered me. Sometimes I couldn't breathe while he was on top of me, my face mashed against the soft flesh of his chest.

When I wanted to break away, I set the house on fire with him locked inside. Sleeping like the baby we never had, he inhaled the black smoke before the flames ever touched his body.

Later, I saw my photograph in the newspaper reports of the fire – the caption under my name that read ARSONIST/LOVER.

"Why did you kill that man?" the boy asks, holding the old newspaper clippings to the interior light.

"Because I had to."

"Would you do it again?"

"If I had to."

"Will you ever have to?"

"I don't know."

"What if you had to kill me?"

"I would rather kill myself," I tell him. "I would go through a burning building if you were somewhere inside and I thought I could carry you away."

"You couldn't carry me."

"Yes, I could."

That's when I tell him to get out of the van. We walk through a patch of dry hot sand into desert. I motion for him to lie down on the parched ground. Leaning over him, I loop one arm under his knees and one under his neck. Then I begin to lift with all my might, straining muscles in my back, neck, legs, and arms. Gritting my teeth so that my skull begins to ache, I feel his body gradually rising. As I lift him off the ground, he's laughing. I feel a sharp pain in my chest where I think my heart might be.

During our first months together, the boy and I drove a winding path. I kept forgetting my troubles every time I looked out the van windows. We passed by cattle and horses ranging in Texas.

We drove away from cornfields to rocky inclines before reaching houses in St. Louis and bridges over industrial rivers. We kept coming back to ocean motels in Galveston, then leaving for tall buildings in dingy cities where houses were stacked close together on hills, old and divided. In Phoenix, skyscrapers rose to smoggy air. In Missouri, we memorized billboards with photos of women smoking, painted angels, and quotations from God bitching about what He had seen on the highway. Large windows reflected the sun and the closer factories that bottled soda and packaged dog food.

Now the boy sits in the front seat next to me. His dog yawns in his lap, then stands on the boy's knees to look out the rainy window. His jeans are coming apart again, ripped at the seams through the red and yellow patches I have sewn across the tatters. The windshield wipers work fast across the glass, but the rain makes trails directed by wind as the drops come together and fly off the windows.

In the rain's distortion, my reflection reminds me of the last time I looked into two-way mirrors. I was ready for the pain to begin. I felt I had to leave Los Angeles before I died there. The man was alive then. He kept pointing out the faint crow's feet at the corners of my eyes and the laugh lines he said made me look sad or cruel, like I was constantly frowning. In the mornings, he told me the pillow lines on my face didn't fade away. He made me afraid I was losing my hair.

"It grows thinner," he said, stroking his chin while he looked at me, "and I find long strands on the bathroom floor."

In the nighttime, he made me wear a wig of dark curls. But he said the wig made me look more attractive than I really was, especially from far away. Occasionally, he let me wander away from the house so he could follow me and spy on strangers I passed by, to prove that my fake hair attracted the wrong type of men. He claimed a large man with coarse hands and a loud voice followed me out of the bar and through the streets to my room. But I was never followed by anyone but him.

He made love to me as if he despised me, throwing me down on the mattress so hard my body bounced under his weight and my head whipped back, injuring my neck. Even now, he's in my memory like bad movies playing in the dark theaters of my childhood, the bone fragments the LAPD found in the house's ashes to trace the fire back to me.

And maybe I don't blame the man for what he did to me, at least not anymore. When he met me, he was a producer at Babie Blu Films Inc. and I was the new star, barely sixteen years old, my fragile light burning away as I undressed on screen. Although I knew what money was mine, I had no idea what would remain private and what the cameras captured when I entered the dim motels. I wasn't like most women I'd known in the business. I escaped it. But even after I left, every building I entered felt like an old brothel newly remodeled and open for business.

Even after he said he wanted to marry me, he still watched the old films of me as a teenager, shivering in the green room night after night where the men stood smoking outside the door.

I wore a lot of blue and purple eyeshadow to make myself look surprised. With the right makeup, I gave myself huge eyes. I wore glittering coffee-colored lipstick to make my mouth look softer. I had to hide the bruises or else I'd go broke.

The boy sits on the bed in the back of the van. The dog rolls out of his coat, slobbering, its sleepy eyes squinting in the lamplight. The boy unwraps his cigarettes, his yellowed fingers rattling the glossy paper. Striking a match on the wall, I light the cigarette he holds in his thin lips.

"Thank you," he says.

"You're welcome." I pick up the dog. It licks my hands.

"Now what can I do for you?"

"What?"

"What do you want from me?"

"Nothing."

He shakes his head and looks at me with mock sadness.

"You're lying," he whispers, his lips pressed to mine.

As for who I was before I became his mother, this is all I know for sure: When I was a young girl, I dreamed of taking over the family business. My father owned a traveling puppet show. I slept with him and my mother in motels or in the back of the van. At night, I could hear my parents making love beside me. The three of us slept so close together there was no way for them to hide what they were doing. I just pretended I didn't hear them.

During the day, we drove from town to town, stopping for whatever churches or daycare centers or elementary schools were in need of an assembly. My father taught lessons with the marionettes, demonstrating how little girls could escape strangers. He also set up a replica of the Milky Way on the stage and started all the major planets turning on strings and wires. Making sure the galaxy stayed in proper position and the strings didn't tangle or break, he helped the children learn where the planets were located as the puppets' spaceship traveled from one planet to the next.

For religious schools, he had a Jesus puppet and a Mary puppet and a Joseph puppet, as well as puppets to represent Samson and Delilah and Adam and Eve. He also had a Satan puppet and puppets of Abraham Lincoln, Einstein, and Hitler. All the puppets had three basic body types – male, female, and child. Their small wigs and clothing were interchangeable, so that the same puppet that represented Joseph could also represent Jesus, Samson, Adam, Lincoln, Einstein, and Hitler. The women were also interchangeable. My father could speak in many different voices, male and female, and he had a voice to fit each character in the puppet show.

When I tried to learn his trade, I failed. It would have taken years and years to learn how to operate the marionettes like my father. When I touched the controls, the strings got tangled around the puppets' bodies, and their arms wouldn't move. My father cursed me because I was no good at changing voices. I was no actress then and no puppet master. It was hardest for me to find a voice for Jesus. I never wanted to make him speak like a man. For some reason, I wanted him to speak to the children in the voice of a young girl.

By the time I turned thirteen, whenever newspapers advertised for figure models, my parents drove me to men who took photographs of me. The white lights of the cameras flashing burned my eyes until I could see only shadowy forms. When I told my mother I was running away to live with the photographers, she said their house was lovely and she wished she could live there with me. But she had to stay with my father, even though she said Babie Blu should send my checks to her P.O. box in Tennessee.

I knew why she wanted me to leave. The van was more cramped than ever, and I was getting too old to sleep so close to my father. Sometimes at night, he reached out for her hair and touched mine by accident, but I don't think she knew what was happening.

A year after I left, the van was found abandoned on an Alabama highway, and my parents were gone. I never heard from them or saw them again. Now their van is all I have to remind me of the life I led with them. I think of my parents whenever I drive through the midnight traffic and wonder where they got lost. When I close my eyes, I see their faces in all this static darkness of newspaper photos fading and think maybe they're dead now or maybe they're searching for me while I search for them. Maybe they've seen me in my films, or maybe we'll never see each other again, never know who we were.

*   *   *

The boy touches my hair. I don't want to hurt him, but I'm afraid to keep him for too long. I'm also reluctant to turn him loose. He has nowhere to go. He has seen me in my saddest moments and is proud of who I am. "Mother," he sometimes whispers, and I can almost believe he is my child. He has already begun to sprout dark hairs on his chest and chin, but he tries to hide the hairs, shaving them off at night with my razor.

I smile at him when he leaves the gas-station bathroom, as if I don't know what he's doing. Perhaps he is already a man and has hidden his age from me all along. Perhaps because he was starving when I found him he appeared younger than he really was, or perhaps I am a bad judge of people's ages. I don't know.

Tonight we sleep on the highway shoulder in the back of the van. In the passing headlights, the boy's eyes remind me of my father's eyes. On the old stage, a long flare of blue turns green and gold as the light turns, winking off and on. There's no way for me to say what the shows were really like unless I close my eyes as I did then and lie still for a long time, my face on a pile of pillows, my hands grasping the soles of my feet. Every time the boy penetrates me, I try to help him reach the dark space behind my eyelids where the others still live. I see my mother and father waiting for me in condemned motels. I see rags on fire and my face burned into the foggy windows.

My father calls to me. He opens his arms as if he expects me to run to him. Somewhere far away I hear my mother crying. A soft sound like muffled laughter goes on too long. The old house is in my eyes. The studio is dark, but when I come inside to look at the old photos, searching the stores for images of my childhood I may have forgotten, the boy turns on the overhead lights inside the van. I see him there, smiling as if he has finally caught me. He has been waiting for me in the dark for so long that his pupils constrict into two black dots like mine.

Whenever I tell the boy that traveling with me is no life for a grown man, he begins to groan and then to whimper, falling at my feet, begging me not to leave him behind. I think he believes there is no better life than the one we lead together, but I don't want him to miss better opportunities. He's a smart boy and will be a handsome man. He could get a good job in a grocery store and have a wife and children.

At night in my dreams, I see the faces of his unborn children watching me through the van windows. When I wake, I tell him what they told me, that he should go to school. But he says no. I am his family. He says there is no woman like me, no woman who can do what I do. No woman knows what I know. I can't argue with him when he says this because it's true: no one in this world understands sex like I do. Moving like a dancer and speaking like a child, I call to the boy in hushed voices I have never spoken before and will never speak again.

Every time I touch him, our arms in the black windows look like oak limbs. My legs open to the stale air. Our faces are pale like the moon at sundown. My makeup is painted like a portrait in an old gallery. In the right light, our bodies are no longer flesh but made of wood and leaves. We gesture to each other like marionettes in delicate motions.

*　　*　　*

When I was a little girl, I sometimes looked at myself in three mirrors at the same time. There was a round mirror in front of my face, a small square mirror in my hands, and a long mirror on the wall behind me. My image ricocheted countless times. I could see my face, my eyes, my hair, and my backside pale and exposed. I was frightened as if I had found other girls naked in my room. But when I turned, my reflections also turned. When I opened my mouth to scream, the other girls opened their mouths. "Who are you?" I kept saying to myself.

Tonight, I am completely nude and standing in front of the bathroom mirror inside an Oakland motel. My makeup mirror is in my hand. I cry until the boy finds me, turning his head away as he wraps me in a white robe.

He leads me back to the bed and covers me in musty blankets. "Baby," he whispers, "baby," as he pulls his black guitar from its case. He strums the silvered strings. I lie down. He sits on the bed beside me and begins to sing a lonely song about a girl who walks on rooftops on rainy nights. He sings about bullfrogs and narrow streets that wind like rivers. He sings me into his songs.

Raccoons and blue wasps travel to houses beside the woods. He sings of waterfalls and old trees, making up the words as he goes along. He can never remember his lyrics from one night to the next, and he plays guitar by ear alone. He can't read music, and he can't read words, so he never writes his songs down. I know every song he sings is a song I'll never hear again.

The guitar was the first gift I gave him. When I offered it to him, we were both sitting in the back of my van, and he was afraid to touch the case. Maybe he thought I was playing a trick on him. I don't know. When he finally took the guitar from my arms, he strummed it gently, weaving odd chords into the strangest song I have ever heard. He didn't know how to play it, but that didn't stop him. He just kept strumming along.

"You keep that," I said. "I never could play it. My fingers are too weak."

He looked at me like he didn't understand my words.

"Keep it. It's yours," I said.

He smiled at me, then looked at the guitar and held it tighter to his chest. Then he put the guitar down behind him, near a mound of quilts where his dog was sleeping. He glanced out the van windows at the night and began to take off his clothes.

"No," I whispered, "not yet."

I drove him to a motel where the highway ended and the ocean began. The van rattled along, the puppets' heads crashing together in their cases every time I made a wrong turn. Because I liked to look at the land as I passed by, I didn't keep my eyes on the road. I was the worst type of driver, constantly chasing the moon from one coast to the other.

"Do you have a cigarette?" the boy asked.

"No." I adjusted the van lights. "But I'll buy you some. I'll buy you lots and lots of cigarettes at the next motel, and I'll steal you all the matches I can find."

He kept quiet for the rest of the way, but he seemed pleased by what I had said. His lips turned up, forming a slight smile that didn't fade away, even when I pulled the van into the empty lot.

In the motel room, sharing a cigarette with him later that night, I was ashamed of myself for the first time in my life – not because of what I had done to him, but because of what he had done to me.

In Hollywood again, after days of driving in circles, taking the same exits on this highway, we finally stop for the night. The motel is claustrophobic with a view of the dark hills. The outside walls are painted yellow, blue, and tan. The lobby has gold wallpaper with green seahorses and orange shells. The carpet is pink with white rows marked by old shoe prints. The boy follows me inside where he immediately finds a cigarette machine. Just like the old days when cigarettes were all he lived for, I empty my purse, my pockets, and wallet to give him all the coins I can find. I have a lot on me. He begins to shove the coins into the slots, his hands trembling in the pale lobby light.

I pay the clerk at the counter. She gives us room number seventeen, and I ask her for matches. I notice she is much older than I am and has pockets of wrinkled flesh hanging from her eyelids and neck. I begin to touch my face slowly, feeling under my eyes. I ask her for more matches, and she empties the entire basket into my purse. The matchbooks are orange and blue with silver marlins etched on their backs. I ask her for twenty dollars in quarters, and I give the quarters to the boy, dumping them onto the table beside the cigarette machine.

I suddenly realize he is much taller than I am, almost six feet tall. He looks down at me and smiles while slipping the quarters into the slots. He puts the cigarette packs and matches into his trench coat pockets and follows me to our room.

Roaches crawl on the white and yellow and pale-blue striped wallpaper and gold tiles in the bathroom. Under the faucets and behind the toilet, a puddle of clear water stands. I have seen worse rooms, and the boy doesn't seem disappointed. But I am. I want to take him to a nicer place, but it's too late.

My makeup kit is already set out on the TV table. In the mirror that faces the bed, we watch ourselves undress. There are pink and yellow perfume bottles, powder in oval boxes, and tubes of red gloss. I reapply my mask, redoing my foundation to even out my skin tone after my evening makeup has been melted by the rain. I put on yellowish concealer to hide the purplish circles under my eyes. I watch my eyes in the mirror as I layer on the blue mascara. Then I watch the boy in the mirror as he watches my eyes. I smile at him and brush on the crimson lip gloss.

"I want to . . ." I whisper.

He looks at me as if I'm not telling the truth. I don't know what the truth is to someone like him. I don't want to know, at least not tonight.

When I put my arms around his neck, he tells a joke I can't understand, something about a vaudeville theater in winter. Even as we hold each other, there's a chasm between us, a brook in a deep valley I don't want to transgress. In silence, he's lost in his own dreams. Every time he looks at me with such forgiveness in his eyes, I feel that I'm becoming a part of those dreams. But I have no idea what he's really thinking. I only know he possesses a calm I've never known.

In the morning, the sky changes colors as I wake in his arms. He pulls me closer, and I trust him more than anyone in the world, more than I've trusted anyone before or since. Now there's nothing I won't let him do to me.

At checkout time, he carries me to the van and lets me sleep in the back while he drives out of the parking lot and onto the highway. I pull the blankets over my face. Even the dim sunlight filtered through the tinted window stings my eyes.

After we've been traveling for less than an hour, he pulls the van off the highway and parks at a rest stop. He settles into the back, sitting next to me. I pull the blankets away from my face to look at him as he runs his hand over the stubble on his chin.

I lie back, opening my legs as I put my hands behind my head. The boy closes his hand and I close my eyes. I feel his knuckles burning against my thigh as he puts his fingers inside me.

When I open my eyes, I look at him as if for the first time. I am confused and feel like he is the adult and I am the child. He keeps pushing until his fingers are gone.

Years go by. I forgive myself but am not forgiven. Although my crime is not forgotten, I am never found. The boy is still a boy. Even though he should have become a man long ago, he never changes. The van breaks down. We repair it night after night, leaving a trail of rusted metal on the dark highway that stretches behind us.

This is not the way our lives were supposed to be, but we go on. There is no future for us. I know that now. He opens his fingers and his hand hurts me. I tell him to go on.

"I'm alive now," I whisper. "I'm alive."

ACKNOWLEDGMENTS

I would like to thank all my writing teachers whose guidance and suggestions have been so valuable to me over the years. And, I would especially like to thank Brian Evenson for encouraging me to develop my own style in writing by teaching the finer points of revision in his workshops. Mark Cox, Lisa Lewis, Maureen McCoy, Lamar Herrin, and Dan McCall are other excellent workshop leaders and writers I was fortunate enough to work with. Thanks to Writers at Work for granting me a fellowship. Thanks to George Oswalt for supplying the cover art for the book. And thanks to my editor, Ted Pelton, who had the vision to begin Starcherone Books in hopes of supporting a few of the risk-takers the big presses left behind. I am grateful to my family for their love and encouragement. Finally, my gratitude goes out to friends and fellow writers whom I've met in various workshops, especially Anna Shapiro and Wah-Ming Chang.

ABOUT THE AUTHOR

Aimee Parkison is originally from Edmond, Oklahoma. She is a graduate of the MFA creative writing program at Cornell University. Parkison has been awarded a Writers at Work fellowship, a prize for emerging writers from *Fiction International* magazine, and the Jack Dyer Fiction Prize from *Crab Orchard Review*. Her stories have appeared in various literary magazines. *Woman with Dark Horses* is her first book.

good books gone bad

FICTION

Starcherone Books

PO BOX 303 Buffalo, NY 14201   www.starcherone.com   publisher: starcherone.com